# WORLDS *Apart*

KATHLEEN KARR

WORLDS *Apart*

MARSHALL CAVENDISH
NEW YORK

Marshall Cavendish
99 White Plains Road
Tarrytown, NY 10591
www.marshallcavensdish.us

This book is a work of fiction. Names, characters, places, and incidents are products of the author's imagination and are used fictitiously. Any resemblance to actual events or locales or persons, living or dead, is entirely coincidental.

LIBRARY OF CONGRESS CATALOGING-IN-PUBLICATION DATA
Karr, Kathleen.
Worlds apart / by Kathleen Karr.
p. cm.
Summary: In 1670, soon after arriving in the Carolinas with a group of colonists from England, fifteen-year-old Christopher West befriends a young Sewee Indian, Asha-po, and learns some hard lessons about survival, slavery, and friendship.
ISBN 0-7614-5195-1
[1. Colonists—Fiction. 2. Survival—Fiction. 3. Friendship—Fiction. 4. Sewee Indians-Fiction. 5. Indians of North America—South Carolina—Fiction. 6. South Carolina-History—Colonial period, ca.1600-1775—Fiction.]
I. Title.

PZ7.K149Wo 2005
[Fic]—dc22
2004019455

*The text of this book is set in Janson.*
*Book design by Michael Nelson*

Printed in the United States of America
First edition
10 9 8 7 6 5 4 3 2

*For Larry—with love and thanks
for your boundless support and belief*

*For more than five hundred years,* the envoys of civilization sailed through storms and hacked through jungles, startling in turn one tribe after another of long-lost cousins. For an instant, before the inevitable breaking of faith, the two groups would face each other, staring—as innocent, both of them, as children, and blameless as if the world had been born afresh.

—Adam Goodheart,
"The Last Island of the Savages,"
*The American Scholar*

*One*

*We came into a new country of inlets and tall pines* and plentiful game in the spring of Our Lord 1670. The ship *Caroline* brought our number, which included my father, Joseph, my mother, Elizabeth, my sister, Julia—and me, Christopher West. The winter seas had not been kind to our party out from England, and I for one threw myself upon the fresh land with gratitude and joy, even going so far as kissing the solidness beneath me. The long-boat from which I had stiffly clambered was pulled in behind me, my family still struggling from it onto the sand. I looked up. Ahead was forest tapering at distant edges into marshland. Forest and—I squinted through the strong noon sun.

*Faces.* Faces—and bodies—blending with the trees, as if they had sprung from their very roots. We were not the first upon this land of Carolina. *Others were here before us.*

Discharging of the vessel's cargo continued through the long, warm afternoon. Heat such as this we had known only from England's midsummers. But in March? Soon we rolled our sleeves above our elbows and even tossed our waistcoats in piles upon the shore. I had said nothing of those faces which had melted back into the primeval forest. What purpose in upsetting my mother and younger sister before our weapons were unloaded?

As the sun set we had tools—if not weapons—in hand at last. We set ourselves to their use, stripping limbs from the nearest trees for posts to hold the canvas that would shelter us this first night. Then we fell into the shelters with complete exhaustion and slept.

It was a strange sound which woke our party with the dawn—a sound I shall never forget. First a humming, then a guttural chant that seemed to come from the earth itself. Tales I'd heard while aboard ship—and pictures etched on maps Father had shown me while still in England—overtook my mind. Visions beset me of races of men who had but a single leg and did not eat but simply drank, creatures with eyes in their shoulders instead of their heads, Amazons who killed their sons and raised only daughters for battle . . . and then there were the *man-eaters*. A shiver shot through my entire being. The visions faded while outside, the otherworldy chorus continued. I turned to my father rolled up beside me. His eyes, wide in wakefulness, mirrored my fear.

"The weapons, Father! The flintlocks, the fowling pieces. The twelve suits of armor! Where are they?"

"Still aboard ship."

With a groan I ripped myself from my coverings and ventured outside the protective canvas. The rising sun greeted me, and a softness in the air I'd never before felt. If death were indeed to be my due, there had never been a fairer day for it. I tore my eyes from the sky and steeled myself to turn toward the forest, toward what I knew had to be emerging from it. *The others.*

Yes, they came. They walked upon two legs. Their eyes were set in the proper places. And they were men as well as women and children. Like us. But they were brown, and their bodies were nearly naked, though their arms were laden. With what? Over their song, over their serenade, my remaining senses began working again. Aromatic odors met my nose. These others were bringing offerings! Far from being *man-eaters*, they carried food. Bowls and trays laden with food. The weakness in my knees overcame me and I collapsed gratefully onto the sand. The people of Carolina were welcoming us.

"Wondrous strange these Indians be," my father proclaimed after he had endured what became known as the stroking compliment. It was the embrace the Indians gave us on that first meeting. As their song changed to whoops it was followed by the greeting:

"*Bony Comraro Angles!*"

We chose to interpret this as meaning, "Welcome, Englishmen!" It had to be a welcome, for the tawny faces shone with wonder, and the naked arms and hands reached out to stroke us on heads, shoulders, bodies.

I accepted the embrace better than my family, it being given by a young man as near to my fifteen years as myself. I admired the necklace of tiny shells decorating his chest, and his deerskin loincloth. He admired the fairness of my hair, my breeches, and the broadcloth of my shirt. Then we breakfasted together on bowlfuls of nuts and root cakes and a curious, warm gruel. Fortunately part of our trade goods had been unloaded, and we could offer brass rings and tobacco in return for the hospitable meal.

My new acquaintance made much of his ring, trying it first upon a toe, before I shook my head and touched his finger. Then he must needs try it on all of his fingers and reached for another—

I held back his hand, but he shook his own head, picked up the new ring, and placed it on my palm. I grinned and slipped it on my finger.

"Christopher." I pointed to myself.

"Asha-po." He pounded his chest.

I held out my newly ringed hand. "Friend."

"Friend?" he asked.

"Asha-po—" I gestured toward him this time. "Christopher—" I pointed again to myself. "Friends."

"*Comraro*. Friend." He reached for my hand.

We both smiled.

*Two*

*By sunset of that first full day in the new land,* I managed to slip away from my family and fellow colonists to walk along the shore. A gentle breeze from the sea cooled the sweat of labor from my body as I was drawn toward a curious tree standing in regal isolation among the dunes. A *palm*, one of the Barbadians in our number had called it. It was composed of a slim, ridged trunk as naked as the Indians' skin—with a topknot of enormous and wildly skewed, serrated leaves. That topknot brought forth an image of the wigs worn by worthies back in London, bringing a smile to my lips, and a chuckle.

"Chris-to-pher."

I spun around. Our Indians had disappeared with their bowls and gifts after the morning meal, leaving me with wandering thoughts all the day. Thoughts of their life, so different from ours; of their speech; their ways—all had swirled through my brain. But always my mind had returned to one Indian in particular. Now he was silently approaching me, as if thinking similar thoughts.

"Asha-po!"

He returned my glad smile with a serious nod before his attention strayed. It became riveted not on me, nor even on the marvelous tree I stood beneath. Instead he stared with every atom of his being at the ships riding at anchor offshore. There rocked the *Caroline* which had transported my family and the other English who'd emigrated. A little farther out sat the *Port Royal*, which had arrived crammed with Barbadians from their overpopulated island. There had been a third ship in our flotilla, the *Albemarle*, long since sunk during a monstrous storm—a *hurricane*—which had beset us off the Leeward Isles. I shivered in remembrance of the fury of the seas, which I had no desire to ever experience again.

Asha-po finally tore himself from the sight with a grunt.

"Canoe." He gestured broadly with both arms, seeking words we could share.

"Big?" I asked. "*Big* canoes. Big *ships*."

"Big . . . ships," he repeated, as if memorizing the words. "Asha-po," he pounded his chest. "Asha-po canoe." He made a small shape.

"Asha-po has *small* canoe," I offered.

He nodded. "Small." He turned toward the west, toward the fading pinks and purples of the sky, then abruptly again to the east, pointing to where the sun would rise.

"Sun," I said. "When the sun rises again. In the morning?" I made rising sun motions.

Asha-po grunted once more. He pointed to the tree, then again to where the sun would rise on the morrow.

"Here," I said. "Christopher and Asha-po *here*, at dawn."

A nod.

I watched him slip away across the sands and into the trees. Dawn. Even though such a meeting might incur my father's wrath, I would be here at dawn.

My father was wellborn, but not highborn. He was a City man—a second son and merchant. Yet he had been charged by the Lord Proprietors of the new Colony of Carolina to oversee the enterprise. He stood in lieu of the appointed governor, William Sayle, who though one of our number was ancient and doddering and not like to live out the year. Each day I discovered some new parts to Joseph West. That night, as I returned to the fires surrounding our makeshift homes, I was to discover more. He had summoned the men to a meeting.

"Christopher West!"

He caught me as I tried to disguise my tardiness by hiding behind the servants of Stephen Bull. Small chance. Even the darkness could not screen his vigilance. "Yes, sir?"

"You will not remove yourself from the safety of our camp!"

"No, sir. Excuse me, sir."

As I wilted into the sand, Father redirected his attention to the group at large. "None of you shall absent yourselves until our palisade is erected and we have better knowledge of the heathens who surround us."

I kept my tongue, but Dr. Henry Woodward, who our party had rescued during that same terrible hurricane—a man who had lived among the Indians—did not keep his.

"These Sewee have made the friendliest of overtures, and I feel certain they be harmless to our enterprise, West. We need only inaugurate trade with them. Their deerskins will go far toward filling the hulls of the *Caroline* and *Port Royal* on their homeward voyages."

"Aye, that and the lumber we'll be felling," John Harleston added.

"'Tisn't *these* Indians we need protection from, as well most of you know," my father broke in. "There be other heathens abroad in the land less amenable to our presence. We've had it on good authority from intelligence offered by the Virginia Company."

He paused to gather fully the attention of the eighty souls before him. "There also be the Spanish."

"They hold sway only as far as Florida," Mr. O'Sullivan declared.

"Would that were so," Dr. Woodward interrupted. "The Spanish tend to see the whole of the continents—North and South both—as their rightful domain and swoop down on new settlements with no provocation. My firsthand experience in Port Royal but three years back proves that. Was I not taken prisoner by them?"

Father held up a hand. "Gentlemen. Yes, we have the Spanish to fear, but it is something worse than the Spanish which chills my heart this night."

His eyes glinted in the firelight as he slowly inspected those surrounding him—English to one side, Barbadians to the other, both with their indentured servants to the rear.

"We accomplished much today, yet it could not pass my attention that some among you chose not to labor to the best of your abilities . . . chose not to continue to work when the perspiration of your labors threatened to drench your fine, linen shirts."

A mumble of protest arose. My father raised his hand again.

"I have called this assembly to speak only the facts. These be the facts: the Colony of Roanoke failed because its gentlemen refused to work. Jamestown almost failed before the gentlemen of that colony *learned* to work. Here in Carolina we shall *all* work, we shall *all* sweat—gentlemen and servants alike—for the common good. For the common interest." He paused to allow his words to settle before proceeding.

"Make no mistake what that common interest is: our mutual gain. Never forget that Carolina can be for us the Land of Milk and Honey, the American Canaan, the new Eden. Never forget that Carolina lies in the same latitude as Aleppo; the same latitude as Peking, the richest city of the Orient—yes, and nearly the same latitude as Jerusalem. Carolina's richness is the future before us, but that richness will not come without sweat."

Father now had the group in the palm of his hand. I had to admire his mastery.

"Ten years hence," he continued, "gentlemen and servants alike will all be independent men. All will have their own allotments of land. All, with their families, will live better than ever was possible in either England or Barbados. Think on this when you raise your saws and axes and hammers tomorrow. Think on this and forget all that separates us. Forget religion; forget birth; forget English or Barbadian. Forget all but the future. Sweat with a *will*."

"Well said!"

"Aye!"

Shouts of approval filled the night sky. I headed for my blanket. More sweat would come soon enough, but before that would come the dawn.

_Three_

_Dawn was a long time coming. After my family_ was safely asleep, I dragged my blanket outside and lay on it gazing up at the stars. I had watched the stars while aboard ship. To allay the tedium of the seemingly never-ending voyage, I'd befriended the sailors of the _Caroline_ and had learned to see the stars as they did, as guides to navigation. I had even learned to read a compass and use a sextant, so knew whereof my father spoke when he mentioned Carolina's promising latitude.

Yet the night sky aboard ship in the midst of the ocean swayed as the ocean did. Here, flat on my back on the sand I had burrowed into, it was suddenly still. Constellations stood out boldly against the Milky Way. The entire universe of stars encompassed me. This universe did not feel cold. It felt more embracing than my blanket.

Never had I seen the night sky exactly this way before. Certainly not in London. In London—even on the best of nights—the sky was blotted out by smoke. Smoke rising from all those chimneys. Smoke rising from . . .

I shuddered at the remembrance overtaking me. It was four years gone, but I would never, could never forget the Great Fire of London. Our maid, Betsy, had woken the entire household at three in the morning by stumbling up the stairs screaming.

"*Fire*! Lord have mercy on us! There's fire in the City!"

Shortly I was standing on the roof with my father watching the dim glow grow before us.

"'Tis at the back side of Mark Lane," Father mumbled to himself. "Not yet anywhere near my warehouse."

My father packed me off to bed again, but in the morning—it was a Sunday, I remember, but no one was readying themselves for church service—I begged him to allow me to accompany him as he set off to inspect the damage. With disaster on his mind, he barely stopped to argue and once outside hardly noted my presence.

Choking vapors drifted through the air, obliterating the usual reek of slops and refuse in the narrow streets. Yet we had no inkling of the true nature of the catastrophe till Father made for the Tower where he tipped the child of a guard to take us up one of the turrets. I scrambled to an opening, then gasped.

"The London Bridge!"

"Only half a mile to the west." Father was squinting through the haze over my shoulder. "Nearly all its houses in flames. And between Thames Street and the river—"

I hoisted myself on the stonework ledge for a better view. "The whole district is blazing! Father, your warehouse is not far off!"

"Yes, the spirits." He stared as one benumbed. "All those barrels of fine Canary and Spanish wines . . . With this wind carrying the fire, there'll be fuel enough to blow it to heaven." He shook his head. "It seems I have built my house upon the sand."

"What of your office in the City? Can it be saved?"

He sighed. "I had best tend to that before it becomes too late. Not that invoices and receipts will stave off ruination. Can you see yourself safely home, Christopher?"

I stood tall within my eleven-year-old frame. "Of course, Father."

"Do so. Tell your mother to begin packing the valuables. The essentials. As quickly as possible."

I raced down the turret steps after my father, heading importantly for home. Father disappeared, but I lingered a moment at the edge of the river. Downstream, householders were flinging their belongings into bobbing lighters. Wait. Some were flinging them into the very river itself! At their backs the fire marched forward, consuming everything in its path. And that path was spreading into many paths before my eyes. Already half of London seemed alight. *Why was no one stopping the fire? Why was no one fighting it?*

Remembering my errand at last, I tore myself from the grisly sight and made my way home.

Sunday turned into Monday, then Tuesday. Still the fire raged. Father's warehouse and office were lost, but our house remained spared. For the moment. We stood packed to leave, but there were neither wagons nor carts to be had for the leaving. I took up my post on our roof. From there I watched the lead of St. Paul's roof pour in rivulets into the churchyard, watched—

"Christopher!"

I tried answering my mother, but coughed instead. Then hacked deeply, feeling the smoky ache spread through my chest.

"Come down at once! Your father has found a boat to take us to Woolwich!"

And so we escaped the Great Fire of London. It continued to rage till week's end. At the last, our house was saved. Father's fortunes were not. That was when he had begun collecting information on the colonies.

I sighed.

A pity he'd not done so earlier. Done so before the London Plague, the year before the Great Fire, had taken my older brother and my youngest sister . . . Jonathan, so like in looks and manner to Father . . . Emily, who danced into everyone's heart.

I blinked, and London disappeared. I was staring at the Carolina stars again. I drifted off as they began to dim.

The shriek of a gull woke me with a start, clearing smoldering dreams from my head. The sun was beginning to edge above the ocean. I tossed off my blanket and ran.

Asha-po!

The first rays of the sun struck silver water. Before me it turned to gold as the Indian's canoe glided smoothly from the mouth of a dune-hidden inlet to pause before me. He set down his paddle and motioned for me to join him. I splashed through the water and did his bidding with little grace. He snick-ered. "Chris-to-pher—"

"Is clumsy," I finished as I sorted out my limbs within the boat.

"Clum-zy?"

I kicked my legs extravagantly and almost suc-ceeded in overturning the canoe. Then I settled down. "Clumsy," I repeated.

"Clum-zy Chris-to-pher." He swallowed another snicker. Then he handed me a second paddle and proceeded to teach me how not to be clumsy.

Asha-po's boat, his *canoe*, was a wonder. I admired it once I'd gotten the benefit of his lessons. The craft was made from a massive, single log that had been burned and scraped hollow. Yet the work had been done with such artistry, and the wood used so buoyant, that the boat was seaworthy. Certainly seaworthy enough to be taking us at this moment in the direction of the colony's anchored ships.

"Big . . . ship." Asha-po pointed ahead, pleased with his words.

"You remembered!" I pointed to my head. "Big . . . ship. Re-mem-ber in head."

He touched his head. "Head." He thrust his hand into the water, then pulled it out dripping a liquid stream, turning to me with a questioning look.

"Water," I said.

He pointed above.

"Sky."

At the rising sun. "Sun?"

"Yes! Sun!" I reached forward to clap him on the shoulder in congratulations.

Asha-po nodded with satisfaction, then concentrated on our route through the slight ripple of waves. We paddled around the *Caroline* with Asha-po pausing to reach out to touch the boards of the hull or to grasp at the thickness of the anchor rope. Finally a sleepy sailor poked his head over the railing.

"Who goes there?"

"Is that you, Sam?"

"Christopher! And—" he rubbed his eyes for a better look. "What be you doing with a heathen, lad?"

"Teaching him English and learning a few things myself."

He stared some more. "Looks as if he'd favor coming aboard."

"May we?"

"Why not? 'Tis weary I am with guard duty, and the day hardly begun. Be hours yet till yon men ashore gather themselves enough to row the long-boats back for more goods."

Sam sent down a rope ladder; we secured the canoe and soon heaved ourselves aboard. Asha-po chose not to speak, but he expelled a continuous stream of interested grunts and disbelieving snorts as I led him through the *Caroline*. When we were done with the tour—all the way down to the holds and back—Sam reached into his pocket and handed something to Asha-po. It was a fistful of the bright trade beads we had brought with us.

Asha-po nodded his thanks, carefully tucked the colorful lot into the pouch around his waist, and indicated he was ready to disembark. He paddled silently back to our palm tree's shore. Once there, he lifted a single finger.

"One. One day," I guessed.

"Sun." He pointed to the tree.

"Dawn—sun—here?"

Asha-po nodded.

I nodded back, slipped my oar into the canoe, and made tracks for my breakfast.

When I set down the broadax to swipe at my forehead that afternoon, I saw the Sewee returning. This time their arms were filled with skins. Father glanced up from the two-handed saw he was sharing with Dr. Woodward.

"Callers coming."

Dr. Woodward smiled and straightened his back. "Good. Best to get started with business as soon as possible." He spoke a few words to the Indians. An old man set down his load and pulled something from his pouch. It was one of Asha-po's trade beads. My disobedience in leaving camp had borne fruit sooner than I'd hoped.

"How in the name of high heaven—" Father began.

"Um." I cleared my throat. "Perhaps I can explain, Father."

"Then do so. Immediately."

Dr. Woodward appeared to be an authority on deerskin. He also appeared to be an authority on Indians. He lined them up and one by one gravely inspected their goods. From a distance I watched in fascination as he remarked on the quality of the tanning, poked his fingers through the odd hole, and slowly built a pile of acceptable skins and another of those rejected. Next he called for our trade goods and began to bargain. It seemed the entire company watched these transactions until Father shook himself out of his own trance.

"We'll never have planks for the palisade," he called out, "if such distractions halt all work."

I reached for my ax as the sounds of labor returned, yet paused for a final search for Asha-po among the Sewee. Only the elders had come. Perhaps he had his own work to attend to. I set to dressing limbs from the felled trunk before me.

"How do you find your meal, husband? 'Tis the very first concoction of my own making . . . ."

Father glanced up from his bowl of venison stew that evening. "Nearly as fine as Cook's back in London, my dear."

Mother blushed with pleasure. "I wrote out Lucy's receipts before leaving, but she had nothing for venison, so I substituted her beef with onions and heavy beer—"

"And I found watercress for the salad in the stream and kept the fire going under the pot!" added my sister Julia. "Have you any idea how hard it is to achieve a 'rolling simmer' on a camp fire?"

The Sewee had brought food this afternoon, too—fresh venison and dried corn. But this time they'd traded it for more English trinkets. They were learning fast.

Father swallowed a bite and waved off the woman talk. "Christopher."

"Yes, Father?"

"Perhaps . . . perhaps your acquaintance with this Sewee boy is not such a bad thing after all. Perhaps it might behoove us for you to pursue—"

"Please, Joseph." My mother's cheeks abruptly paled from her blush. "It frightens me. They frighten me."

"We must learn to live with them, Elizabeth."

"May I learn to live with them, too?" Julia piped up. "There was a girl my own age yesterday morning—"

"Absolutely not!" Father roared. He took a moment to settle himself. "I'll not have my women endangered."

Mother tugged at a loose lock of her flaxen hair. "But your son—" she tried again.

"Christopher is nearly a man—the only of such age among our company. He must aid our endeavor in whatever manner best suits our needs. And our current needs include fresh meat. We cannot be bartering our limited trade goods for food when there is obviously so much of it about." He eyed me carefully. "If I were to give you leave of your other duties—"

*Yes*, I breathed within myself. *Oh, yes.*

"—can you be trusted to do some exploration of this subject? Hunting methods and patterns, other intelligence that could prove useful to us . . ." Father stared at me.

I forced myself to calmly dip my spoon into the stew. "Certainly, Father."

He nodded.

The food lumped in my stomach as I struggled to give no sign of my jubilation. With the fresh dawn would come *freedom*. I was being given freedom to explore this new land. With Asha-po. What had London—what had all of England—to compare?

*Four*

*In haste to begin my new life, I found myself* waiting under the lone palm much too early. Sometime in the course of the night a fog had settled over the sea. I peered through its grasping tendrils, stamping my feet with impatience. When would the sun break over the horizon? Would it burn off the fog? If it did not—if the rising sun hid behind a bank of clouds—would Asha-po not come?

This terrible possibility led to other reflections. Did Asha-po consider it a day when the sun was not shining? . . . How did he really *think*? How could I break into his mind with such a pitiful few words to share?

Almost on the point of despair, I heard a slight, swishing sound. A raised paddle cut through the cottony miasma, sprinkling drops of water onto the still surface of the sea.

"Asha-po!"

The bow of his canoe hove toward me, and I didn't wait for an invitation to leap into it behind my friend.

"Chris-to-pher."

He turned to acknowledge my presence. Anxious as I was to communicate, I attacked the language problem immediately, pointing toward the horizon. "*No* sun."

He wrinkled his brow. "*No?*"

I ran a hand through my damp hair in frustration. How to explain a negative? The concealed sun gave me a clue. I pointed to my face. "Christopher *head.*" Then I covered my face with my hands. "*No* Christopher head." Finally I pointed to the east where the sun refused to appear. "*No* sun."

Asha-po's own face was a study as he struggled with the idea. It wasn't working. My description had been closer to *hidden.*

"*Zoons!*"

In frustration I thrashed at the water surrounding us. Then I gave the water a second look. . . . This was a word he understood. I cupped a handful. "Water," I said.

"Water." He nodded.

I let it dribble from between my fingers. Raised my empty hand. "*No* water."

"No water." Asha-po stared at my hand, then

reached over the canoe for a handful of his own. "Water—" He tossed it overboard and cupped his empty hand again. "*No* water," he declared. He pointed toward the hidden sun. "*No* sun!"

"*Struth*." I swiped at my perspiring brow. This language business was heavy labor. Maybe it were best to let it proceed more naturally and return to the morning's affairs.

"Big ships?" I asked.

"No big ships. *No* sun." He gestured at the fog.

"Fog," I explained.

"Fog." Asha-po accepted.

He pivoted the canoe and made for the inlet from which he had appeared. Within minutes we had entered another world. The ribbon of sand was behind us, and we made a passage through endless acres of low marshland alive with numberless fowl. The cacophony of their cries muted as trees closed in and the inlet became a river. We paddled silently through a landscape of pale greens and grays, broken only by the swoops of brilliantly emerald-and-yellow parrots. I watched Asha-po lift his oar to let the boat drift and followed his lead. He nodded slightly ahead and to the right.

"*Aaaah . . . .*" I breathed a whisper of awe.

A deer stood but twenty yards before us, neck strained in alertness. A doe it was, with two fawns beside her, lapping from the river. Only once had I seen such graceful creatures. It was some months before our expedition was set to embark. My father was still organizing matters and in the absence of his eldest son had taken me with him to the estate of Lord Ashley, one of the Proprietors. It was two days' journey from London by carriage. Coming from the tight confines of the city, I could scarcely believe the estate's vast acreage when we entered the gates. The park surrounding Ashley's castle—for it certainly seemed such to me—had mown fields, formal gardens, and its own lake encircled by follies. These tiny, fanciful buildings in the Greek and Italian styles delighted me. But even better, Lord Ashley's estate encompassed its own forest, with its own herd of deer.

"Private, of course—" Father commented as we took the air within its tidy confines, "—as are all forests within England. They belong either to the nobility or to King Charles himself."

"This I know, but in Carolina, Father?" I asked.

"The forests will belong to *us*. No wood fees to pay—" He stopped short as a stag bolted across our path. He stared as its antlers disappeared into the foliage. "Free hunting for all, not just the highborn. No death penalty for poaching, as there will be no poachers." A smile softened my father's grave face. "All will be free men of property."

I let out my breath as the doe gave a nervous jerk

and skipped back into the forest with her young ones. I was in a land Lord Ashley could never dream of, nor understand, back on his ordered estate. Asha-po dipped his paddle again, and I followed suit. Deeper into the wilderness we floated.

How could I describe the marvels I was seeing to my father? The deer: there were more to be seen, many more, all vanishing with a flick of their white tails. . . . The great bear fishing for his breakfast, scarcely glancing up as we skimmed past. In England I had only known bears tethered in London's gambling pits. . . . Foxes and wild turkeys—the bounty of creatures almost sated me. Also catching my fancy was the strange vegetation that drifted onto our shoulders from overhanging boughs as we slid beneath. I reached for a long strand, marveling at its mossy texture. I was still marveling when Asha-po leaned back and prodded my arm.

"What?" I asked.

He pointed next to us. In the river's shallow water a log greater than the canoe's length floated alongside. I bent closer. A strange sort of a log it was. . . . It seemed almost to be keeping pace with us. I raised an eyebrow at Asha-po. In answer, he lifted his paddle and gently tapped it.

"*Aargh!*"

I leaped back on my haunches. A head was rising!

A horrible head! With beady eyes to either side of armored skin . . . Now its mouth yawned open—

"*Teeth!*" I yelped. "Rows of *big*, huge *teeth*—"

Asha-po roared and plunged his paddle into the water till we were well ahead of the abomination.

I waited for the shudders in my body to cease. "What?" I finally asked.

Asha-po was still fighting a grin. "*Alligator.*"

I formed my mind around the syllables. "Al-li-ga-tor." My Indian friend had taught *me* a word!

Asha-po knew it, too. He pointed to a tree. "What?" he asked.

"Tree," I answered. "That . . . is . . . tree."

He splashed at the river. "That . . . is . . . water."

A ray of sunlight broke through the mists surrounding us. We both pointed.

"That is **sun!**" we crowed.

The world expanded like rays of the sun. Simply. Naturally. Truly, the light of understanding is a wondrous, joyful gift.

The weeks that followed my first encounter with the wilderness were busy ones. It was a satisfaction to watch the encampment's primitive tents give way to sturdier huts, to watch the palisade's walls form, but a far greater satisfaction to learn the lore of the forests under Asha-po's guidance. Would that I'd had such a teacher in London! Would that I'd had such living books! But the past was history, and I was grateful when, only a few days after my first journey into the heart of the wilderness, Asha-po officially became my new master.

"Chris-to-pher." He tied fast our canoe to a bough, beckoned me ashore, then leaned back into the boat for a long, skin-wrapped parcel. He carefully revealed its contents.

"Bow," I noted. "Arrows."

Asha-po grunted. "Bow." He handed it to me. "Ar-rows." He presented a filled quiver, then reached into the canoe again for his own set.

I stared dumbly at the weapons.

Asha-po shook his head and tried again. "Asha-po *bow*." He gestured with his. Pointed to mine. "*Chris-to-pher* bow."

Enlightenment dawned. "It's a *gift*! Asha-po give Chris-to-pher bow gift!"

"*Gift*. Bow. Ar-rows. Asha-po, Chris-to-pher hunt."

"Yes! We hunt!"

But first I admired my new treasures. The bow was my height, as if made for me, and finely crafted from a single piece of ash. It had been lovingly polished. I traced the satiny grains with trembling fingers. *My first weapon.* I forced it aside to examine an arrow from the quill: squinted down its length as I'd seen men do in our encampment. It was straight shafted and would fly true. I cautiously touched its bone point—razor sharp. And the feathers! The arrow was skillfully fletched with a brilliant rainbow of feathers.

"*Zoons!*" I grinned at Asha-po. "Wonderful bow! Beautiful arrows!"

A raised eyebrow told me my adjectives were too much. I added, "Thank you!" anyway.

Asha-po grunted and turned to business. He demonstrated how to bend the bow and tighten its string of sinew. That accomplished to his satisfaction, he tossed the full quiver at me and led the way into the forest. I followed—until he suddenly spun, pointing at my boots with a scowl.

"Boots," I blithely translated. "What?"

"*Boots.*" Asha-po hissed the word. He pantomimed boots crashing into the undergrowth.

"Oh." I studied the villains. "Boots bad. Boots *noisy*." I clumped a few noisy steps. "Noisy."

"Noy-zy," Asha-po agreed. He mimicked deer fleeing.

I bowed reverently over my boots. Father had had them fashioned for me—in top-grain cowhide— before we'd left England. They had seen me all the way across the Atlantic Ocean. I twitched my toes within their solid squareness. . . . Maybe they *were* becoming a bit small. With a sigh, I bent to unfasten the buckles and tug them off. A snicker followed.

"*What?*" I asked Asha-po.

He held his nose and pointed at my heavy, woolen socks.

"Well, if you'd been living in them for a few weeks, your socks would reek, too!" I sank to the ground and yanked them off.

"*Socks.*"

I exhibited the articles for Asha-po's edification. Alas, I waved the pair too near my nose. "*Struth!*" I gagged. "Worn a week too long, I think."

Watching my face, Asha-po clutched his stomach and hooted. After I had tucked boots and socks into my shoulder bag and struggled upright, he fought another hoot of mirth.

"What *now?*" I was beginning to feel distinctly put upon.

Asha-po pointed to my feet and erupted anew.

"*Feet,*" I translated. Then I glanced down at them. *White. Pasty.* Looked at his. *Brown. Tough.* Asha-po owned working feet. I stiffened my spine.

"Christopher make feet good. Like Asha-po feet."

He wiped the remaining grin from his face, nodded, and set off once more. I limped in painful pursuit.

I was not destined to bag my first deer that day, nor for many after. First I must learn to glide silently through the forest like a Sewee. . . .

◊        ◊        ◊

"*Clum-zy* Chris-to-pher!"

"Sorry—" I looked up from the root that had just tripped me flat, causing a mass exodus of birds and squirrels, "—again."

He shook his head as I raised a foot and studied its sole. Calluses were developing, but not nearly fast enough. This latest blunder had left another bloody gash. I sighed. Asha-po did, too. Then he disappeared into the underbrush to return with a fistful of odd-looking leaves. Carefully bruising them, he spat and worked the mess into mush. When satisfied with its consistency, he applied the poultice to my latest wound and bound it all together with broad leaves and vine. I rose and gingerly put pressure on the foot.

*Struth*. No pain! "Good!" I told my friend.

He shook his head again. "Chris-to-pher *look*." He made circles around me demonstrating his usual stealthy stride once more: controlled breathing, limbs loose but contained, eyes everywhere at once.

"Christopher will learn." I gritted my teeth and had another go at attaining his lithe perfection.

Next I must learn to read the signs of game: the droppings, the nibbled branches, the hair from hides rubbed against tree trunks. . . .

◊        ◊        ◊

"Deer!" I proclaimed. "And fresh." I pulled my twitching nose from the moist droppings and edged back on my knees to glance up cockily at Asha-po. "Same size—" The specimens were just under two inches. "Same shape." The convolutions were curiously brain shaped. I proudly tossed my head. Had I not studied the proper methodology of scientific observation? In this matter I could excel.

Asha-po's face was unreadable. "Track," he ordered.

I studied the heavy dust beyond the lump of dung. Curious . . . a series of light marks about six inches apart . . . followed by flat, broad pad prints. . . . Ignoring vague doubts stirring within, I silently pursued the trail for some yard on hands and knees. So anxious was I to please my teacher that soon I'd scrambled headfirst into a hollow log. Still, alarms did not sound. Never did I stop to consider what a deer with strange tracks might be doing hiding in a large, hollow log—

"*Zoons!*" I was under attack! I leaped back, face *burning*—

Asha-po shoved me aside, reached into the log, and hauled out—

"*What?*" I groaned, gaping with tearing eyes at thirty pounds of bristles.

"Porcupine," he answered, swiftly slicing his knife into the ungodly creature's stomach. "*Dead*

porcupine." He cleaned his gift knife, the knife I had
given him in gratitude for the bow. "Asha-po mother
happy. Sew quills on robes."

"But—" I cried.

"Porcupine trickster. Droppings like deer. Track
*not* like deer."

I stared down my nose at the quills painfully
piercing my cheeks and neck. "I failed your test!"

"Good lesson. Look more next time." He stowed
the porcupine in his game bag and hunkered down
to remove the spines of my agonizing lesson.

While I progressed in this Sewee apprenticeship, the
small wooden fortress of our English colony grew
larger. I took greater interest in this palisade as my
conversations with Asha-po grew in length and com-
prehension.

I was constantly amazed by my friend's daily
advances in English—as he was when I grasped new
words and phrases of his language. We had settled
into a blend of English and Sewee. The mixture may
have sounded odd to most ears, but bothered Asha-po
and me not a whit. Did it not give us shared ideas?
Shared fears, too.

Imagine, then, my utter surprise on learning the
greatest fear in Asha-po's mind. It was not the
Spanish. It was other *Indians*.

He laid bare this anxiety the morning he welcomed me to his village, at last. Coming from the shadows of the forest into the sudden brightness of the clearing, I had to stop and shade my eyes. Slowly I began to register what surrounded me. The Sewee's dwellings were made of thatch. A number of these surrounded a much larger building fashioned more sturdily of clay. It, too, had a thatched roof. As I studied it, Asha-po explained its function.

"For chief, *cacique*. Much talk."

"Ah. A council house, for meetings."

That mystery solved, I turned my attention elsewhere. Filling the remainder of the clearing were several storehouses next to fields being prepared for planting—and scattered between the village and the farmland were Asha-po's people. Women and girls worked the fields. Men squatted before doorways playing at games or lazily fashioning arrows.

"It looks peaceful," I said.

"Now," Asha-po answered.

"What do you mean?"

He counted on his fingers. "Seven. Seven moons ago—"

"Seven *months* ago?"

A nod. "Bad Indians. *Westo*. Chase Sewee from hunting ground—" He pointed toward the forest beyond his village.

"To the north?"

"Yes. Three-day walk *north*. Very much game.

But Westo very fierce. Hunting ground of Sewee not enough. Come here, steal corn, burn village."

"You built again, planted again," I said.

"Yes. But fear here." He pounded his chest.

"Fear in your *heart*."

Asha-po gestured toward the idling men. I noticed what I had not before. Next to each lay weapons—bows and arrows, hatchets, clubs, and spears—at the ready.

"Warriors guard village," Asha-po continued. "You come. English come. Sewee happy. Westo come again, English have guns. Help Sewee."

"I begin to understand."

And I did. From the first, my father's primary mission for me in the wilderness had been to procure food. Asha-po's lessons in woodsmanship had done more than toughen the soles of my feet. They had also taught me stealth, and daily I progressed in the use of my bow—yet I had brought but one deer home for the pot. I'd had greater hopes for the traps Asha-po had taught me to set among the wildfowl of the marshland—yet *they* rarely gathered more than weasel-like creatures with rich pelts but unappetizing flesh. In short, brilliant success as a hunter eluded me.

I had also addressed Father's secondary mission: I had mapped prime game areas for the colony's hunters. Still, it grated to see them clumsily and noisily set off into the forest with flintlocks. With my new skills and a *flintlock*, I knew I could become a better provider, knew I wouldn't waste the colony's small supply of powder and shot. . . .

There remained my father's final directive: to obtain useful intelligence.

I studied the Sewee guards again. There was a certain coiled intensity about them, like great cats ready to spring. The Westo were a serious threat.

"Thank you, Asha-po. For speaking your fear."

I set off for the colony at once. Here was information more important to my father than food. The Westo were likely to attack sooner than the Spanish. I counted back seven months. They had raided last year at harvest time. That was when they would return.

I found my father overseeing the work on the growing palisade. I made my report, then lingered beside him as he digested the news. Slowly he raised his eyes to the raw-boarded walls.

"Will this be enough protection?" I asked.

Father shrugged. "True 'tis small, but the star shape will give us vantage points from five positions—"

"And we've only completed three," I said. "What if the Westo return before September?"

"Less talk, more work, Christopher." He presented me with a hammer.

"Yes, sir." I drove in one of our precious nails.

*Five*

*A ritual circling of the Caroline and the Port*
Royal began each fair new day for my friend and me.
It was hard to understand the trance that overtook
Asha-po on these early morning forays. Some days
he would remain silent in thought until we reached
the shore. On others, he would ask questions.

"The Great Water?"

"The Atlantic Ocean?"

"Yes. It goes far?"

"Very far."

"How many days paddle . . . find England?"

"On the big ship, with sails, it took many moons,
many months to come here. The wind, the waves.
Terrible storms. It depends on them."

A grunt, and Asha-po would sink back into his
thoughts, ignoring my very existence. Just as my

brother Jonathan used to do. Yet once ashore, Ashapo's attention quickly returned to things of the land.

One perfect morning, he absolutely skimmed through the marsh.

"Our traps?" I asked, for we'd taken to checking them early each day.

"Tomorrow," he answered. "Today—" he broke into a rare smile, "—today, is corn-planting ceremony. In my village. Important. *Big*." He smiled again. "Chris-to-pher come. Chris-to-pher my friend, my—"

"Guest?"

"Yes. *Guest*."

"Why?" I asked. "Why corn planting ceremony?"

He gave me one of those looks that were appearing with greater frequency as we learned more about each other. I was beginning to interpret them as, *You foolish English! You understand nothing!* But he answered seriously.

"Corn feeds us. Is good to give thanks."

The Sewee village was alive with preparations. The women were dressed in their finest deerskin robes, decorated with shells and quills and an occasional trade bead. Their hair shone a lustrous black, and care had been taken with its braiding. Men gathered tight-skinned drums. Dogs yipped between the legs of excited children. All was happy chaos till two figures emerged from inside the council house. They stood by its portal, a halo of importance emanating from them. I raised a questioning eyebrow at Asha-po.

"Big man is chief. Sipio. Small man is Kenato. Healer. Make medicine."

I stared at the medicine man. Bead-like marks were painted across his forehead, and a feather loomed from his hair. A leathern bag was slung from his shoulder. As I tallied these details, he stepped forward. Raising his arms to the heavens, he gathered the Sewee. A chant rose from his throat:

"*E ya hai ya no o ha e ya . . .*"

Around me drums began to pound out a rhythm. The tempo began simply, then became more intricate. It was strangely hypnotic. I reached within me for its meaning. The beat of my heart . . . the beat of the land . . . perhaps the beat of the universe itself.

Kenato's chant continued, surrounding the rhythm of the drums, adding a melody to the music. At first I could make little sense of his sounds. Slowly I came to understand that they were not meant as words. They were meant to be experienced, to expand on the drums' beat. They were meant as the sigh of the wind . . . the flow of the river . . . the song of birds. Kenato was singing *life*.

Beside me Asha-po picked up the chant in time with his neighbors. His body rocked, and his legs moved into a dance as natural as the melody. Taking the lead, the swaying Kenato led the Sewee people toward the waiting fields.

Tiny mounds sprinkled the earth. I knelt over one. A single kernel of corn had been carefully tucked inside. Straightening again, I watched Kenato dip into his pouch. His fingers emerged covered with a fine powder. Singing his way through the fields, he blessed each mound with this powder. But now his song became words. These words Asha-po breathed into my ear.

> *Rows of little hills I see,*
> *waiting, waiting.*
> *Corn, much corn,*
> *In our earth mother*
> *We lay to rest.*

> *Our earth mother's living waters*
> *will fall—*
> **Sing thanks, oh people!**
> *Our sun father's bright rays*
> *will surge up from the sea—*
> **Dance joy, oh people!**

> *Corn will rise up standing;*
> *to all directions*
> *Will it stretch its arms,*
> *That Sewee may always live.*

Kenato bent to breathe on a mound.

*I add to your breath. With thanks I do this.*
*May you and your brothers be blessed with light.*

Kenato rose once more and resumed his chant. It became falling rain, then the still moment of the sea as the sun broke over the horizon at dawn. I knew this with certainty. Had I not lived that moment many times with Asha-po?

After the blessing, as in a daze, I flowed with the drums and the dancers back into the village. I danced around cook fires laden with pots of cornmeal mush. Danced around flat, heated rocks sizzling with corn cakes. Shared with the other men Kenato's blessing pipe. Feasted late into the afternoon. Staggered home with the Sewee's gift basket of hard, shelled corn for our own colony's planting.

We had arrived in the planting season. In addition to the immediate needs of shelter and security and food, it was necessary to create a garden for winter provisions. In this matter Asha-po took much interest. Perhaps the corn ceremony had sparked this in him—as it had in me. Several days after his village's ceremony, I led him back to see the changes in our encampment.

He nodded grave approval at the fast-growing palisade walls. "Westo no like."

Next he paused to poke at the worn canvas atop the nearest hut. "No good," he commented. "Big rain come, rain become *guest*."

His use of the word made me smile. "An unwelcome guest." I considered his meaning more carefully. "Heavy rain will come?" I asked. "When?"

"With big heat."

"We name it *summer*, when the big heat arrives."

"In summer. Much rain, and—" He made booming sounds.

"Thunder? Thunderstorms?"

"Many."

I poked at the canvas myself. "We'll need better roofs, then."

"Roof like Sewee. Rain dances away."

I liked that image of the dancing rain, but not dancing on my head. I would have to convince my father to send a few men to the marsh to collect reeds. One of the indentured servants had been a thatcher back in England. With his help, it would be possible to have snug homes.

We wandered behind the collection of buildings to where the trees cleared for lumber had provided a few acres for planting. Asha-po studied the seeds sitting in sacks, waiting to be sewn. He picked up a few, bit into them, and frowned.

"What is wrong?"

"Where corn Sewee give?"

"My mother has it." I gestured across the field to

where Mother and Julia bent over their hoes with the other women. Seeing them like that made me smile. Back in London my fine mother never would have dreamed of dirtying her hands. Back in London my little sister thought only of fancy clothing. Now their fair faces were burned and peeling from the unaccustomed sun. A few less skirts and they would begin to look like Sewee women.

I shook the picture from my head. As for the garden itself, it wasn't yet much—just bare, sandy land set within a protective deer fence. While I was dallying with these thoughts, Asha-po took off across the field. I dashed after him, knowing my mother's fears. Not only my mother's, either. The other women dropped their hoes and scattered at his approach, becoming just so many frightened sparrows. Only Julia staunchly watched from a distant row as Asha-po reached Mother before she could take flight. He pointed to the Sewee basket still waiting, filled with unplanted kernels.

"Corn," he explained. "For you." He fetched a handful and offered it.

"But—" Mother backed away, then spied me and stiffened, ramrod straight. "Christopher?"

"Listen to Asha-po, Mother. It's important."

"Corn," he repeated. "Sweet and soft in summer."

Asha-po thrust the handful at her. I held my breath till Mother finally accepted the kernels. As I exhaled with relief, Asha-po made grinding motions.

"Grind?" Mother managed to ask.

"Grind. For meal in cold time. Plant *now*." He made fast motions.

"Quickly?"

"Quick. Plant now." Asha-po turned to me.

"I will teach her," I said.

"Good. Teach plant." He paused. "Teach . . . how give thanks."

"We will remember to give thanks."

"*Re-mem-ber*." Asha-po's black eyes caught my blue ones. Satisfied that I had grasped the significance of his message, he turned and like one of the forest animals—like a fine stag—bounded over the fence and disappeared into the waiting trees.

"*Christopher*." Mother heaved a long sigh. Next she rubbed the sweat of her labor, and perhaps of her fear, from her forehead. "Would you care to cast more light on all of this?"

"Summer is coming fast, Mother. The Sewee understand this. We've got to plant this corn of theirs."

"But I'm still working on the peas—"

"Asha-po thinks the timing is really critical. I believe him."

Mother eyed me. "You would. You begin to look more like a heathen each day. Barefoot. Shells around your neck. No shirt on your back. Shall I expect to see you next in a loincloth?"

Julia dashed up, eyes sparkling, to catch the end

of Mother's diatribe. "*Ooh*. If Christopher gets to wear a loincloth, may I rid myself of these skirts? Or at least shorten them? There were no fields to plant in London and they do get in the way—"

Our mother opened her mouth—I suspect to scream—but I forestalled her.

"Julia is beginning to understand, Mother. In the wilderness clothes just do *not* matter. The Indians understand this, too."

Mother heaved another sigh and stared at her fistful of corn. "His words about giving thanks . . . what did that mean?"

I gently reached for my mother's chin and caught her eyes. "It means your heathens are not really heathens, Mother. They believe in God as we do. They just call Him by different names. I'll leave the wording of prayers for a successful harvest to your own devising."

"Oh, Christopher!" My mother shook her head free and pulled me into a tight hug, bare chest and all. "This is such a strange land!"

Julia bent for the corn scattered from our mother's fist. "You'd best show us the proper way, the *Sewee* way to plant corn, brother dear."

*Six*

*The day arrived, as it had to, when the Caroline and* the *Port Royal* embarked on their homeward voyage. Asha-po and I sat in his canoe watching anchors being hauled in, watching sailors scurry up the masts to set sails, watching as the wind billowed the sails into life.

"Big ships fly now," Asha-po spoke. "Like birds. Free."

"Yes."

Around us the water hosted other Sewee canoes. Their occupants waited in silence, showing none of the emotions they felt. Behind us on the shore it was a different matter. The entire colony had abandoned its tasks for the leave-taking. Women held handkerchiefs to their eyes. Men bellowed final messages. Youngsters played among them, shying pebbles into the waves, setting gulls into flight.

I turned my sight from the new land back toward the ships. Already they were moving into the endless horizon. Already they were diminishing. Soon the tiny flotilla would be gone from sight. Gone with it would be the illusion of security its handful of puny cannons had given us. Gone with it would be our last connection to our motherland. Our last connection to England. Already I could feel the strangeness of Carolina expanding into the unknowable vastness of the continent hovering in wait. . . .

"Big ships come again?"

Asha-po's question brought me back with a shudder. His eyes had never left the shrinking forms.

"Maybe not these big ships, but others will come."

"When?"

I shrugged. "Soon, I hope."

"Soon mean one moon, two moons?"

"More."

Of that I was certain. Father said the Lord Proprietors had toyed with the idea of sending an interim relief ship, but the matter had not been settled before we'd left England. Very likely they would wait for the return of this little fleet. They would wait until they learned what profit was to be made from the cargo of timber and skins. Until then we were truly alone.

All night long Mother and Julia sniffled in their cots across the tiny one-room hut from me. Their stifled sobs were hard to ignore.

During our meal the next evening—fish I had caught with one of Asha-po's hand-carved lures—Father paused in the midst of boning his portion. "I have decided to build a proper house for you, Elizabeth."

Mother's head jerked up. Her eyes were still rimmed with red. "When?"

"We will begin in the winter, after the harvest and when all has been made secure for the colony at large."

"Where?" I asked.

"On the banks of the Ashley River, where I have made the decision to take up my lands. Your one hundred acres, too, of course, Christopher."

"The *Ashley* River, Father? Do you mean the *Kiawah*?"

He snorted. "It will now and for all future time be known as the *Ashley*."

"In honor of Lord Ashley, I suppose. I wonder what the Sewee will think about that."

"Of course in honor of Lord Ashley, Christopher. I sent a letter by the *Caroline* explaining it. Explaining other matters as well. Among the Proprietors, Lord Ashley is the most interested in our colony. The enthusiasm of the others fades with their age."

I couldn't help but notice my father's complete indifference to what the Sewee did or did not think. I decided to test him on another issue.

"I'm not certain I want my land so close to the water. I might choose elsewhere to avoid the mosquitoes." I slapped at one buzzing around my head. They had multiplied with the warming season. Father's knife paused again.

"While you eat at my table, you will conform your wishes to mine."

"We eat at this table because I bring the food," I snapped back—a truth daily more apparent as my hunting and fishing skills improved.

My father's cheekbones tensed. "Your brother would not have answered me thus."

"Jonathan is dead, Father." I slapped my knife onto the rough planks of the table. "I am only the second born. Like you."

Color rose in Father's face.

Mother grasped at her handkerchief. "Please—"

"If this insolence is the result of too much liberty among the heathens," Father roared, "that liberty shall stop!"

I had overstepped myself. With Jonathan gone, primogeniture—by English law, exclusive inheritance by the eldest son—now fell on me, but the stigma of being considered second best still rankled. Obviously it held true for my father as well. "I beg your pardon, Father." I bowed my head. "The departure of the ships has affected me, too."

Through lowered lids I waited for my father's response.

"So it has." He smashed at a cloud of mosquitoes. "The palisade is nearly finished. Perhaps with that accomplished you might care to give me a tour of land you consider more beneficent to our needs."

"It would be an honor, Father."

Beside me Julia reached for my hand beneath the table and gave it a squeeze. Mother tucked away her handkerchief. The meal resumed.

Asha-po and I still met by the lone palm. Once I was secure in the canoe he would aim its prow toward the sea, toward where the ships had sat at anchor. For long minutes he would contemplate their absence. I waited in silence, watching his fingers curled around the paddle, knowing the exact moment they would tighten to sweep it once more through the water for our return to the land.

It was the land that now began calling to me as the sea did to Asha-po. One hundred acres of it were to be mine—and many more acres would fall into my father's keeping. Coming from the narrow tightness of London, it was a largesse hard for me to conceive. It was also hard for me to conceive that King Charles and his Lord Proprietors so many thousands of miles away could have assumed that all this land—all of Carolina and more—actually belonged to *them*.

It had never entered their noble minds that Sewee and Westo and other tribes already lived in this far country. It had never occurred to them that Indians had owned this land first. This was not a thought that troubled my father or any of the other colonists, either. It troubled me.

As I roamed the marshlands and forests with Asha-po, I began to wonder where the Sewee's territory began and ended. I began to wonder which tract I could choose that would not take something from my friends. One afternoon, as we explored a piece of forest new to me, I posed this question to Asha-po. At least I tried.

"Asha-po—" I sprawled on a log and set down my quiver of arrows and bow. It was my gift bow, the weapon which had given me my first deer. My second and third, too. Asha-po squatted before me and pulled his knife from its sheath—the gift knife which had slashed into my porcupine's soft underbelly. He began playing with it.

I watched him flip the blade lithely into the air, again and again. Jonathan flashed into my mind. . . . Jonathan playing mumblety-peg in our London garden before he became sick. Me begging to join his game. Jonathan refusing. Always refusing my friendship . . . Light flashed on the steel blade as Asha-po caught it in midflight and sent it flying into the bark of a tree twenty feet away. There it stuck fast. My friend grinned before turning sober.

"Three days, four days. I watch your head. I see spirit troubled."

I banished Jonathan to the past and pointed to my head. "My head holds my hair and my eyes, my ears and my nose and my mouth. Inside my head is my *mind*. My mind thinks. My mind is troubled."

"Ah." He considered. "English think spirit comes only from inside head. From inside *mind*."

"Maybe." There was also the soul to consider, and it was probably what Asha-po really meant. Perhaps *soul* was the same for him as *spirit*. John Hawkes, my tutor back in London, could have finely split the words, then tied them into knots with his philosophical lectures. I regretted losing my brother before we had had the chance to become friends. I did not regret the lost lectures.

"What troubles me, Asha-po—" I tried again, "—what *worries* me, is the land."

"Land?" His face went blank.

I motioned around us. "The trees, the marsh, your cornfields. Everything."

"How this be trouble? It is good."

"Of course it is good. It is wonderful!"

"How then trouble?" He stretched his head back to catch the patch of open sky above us. "Sun father smiles. Corn grows. In trees, birds sing. What is bad?"

I tugged at my hair in frustration. It had grown to my shoulders, almost as long as Asha-po's. Another tug, and I decided to start over, from the moment of our arrival. "When we English came, you gave us food; you gave us corn to plant. You taught me to hunt."

He nodded.

"My people cut down trees to make houses. Cut down trees for fields to plant corn."

"English need village, too. English must eat."

"Yes, but can't you see, don't you understand—" I deliberated over the critical words, then plunged in. "The trees we cut, the fields we plant our corn in, all belong to the Sewee. All are the *property* of your people."

Asha-po shrugged. "What is *property*? There are many trees, much land."

"But my people will cut down many more trees. Many, *many* more."

"Why?"

"To make bigger fields for growing. And they will hunt more deer, too."

"How much can an English eat? He cannot swallow from so many fields. Too much deer make him sick." Asha-po rubbed his stomach.

"The extra corn will be sent to England, to feed the people there. The skins of the deer will follow those skins already in the big ships, to make clothing for the people in England."

Asha-po's eyes widened. "So many people live in England? More than Sewee?"

I nodded. "More than the Sewee. More than the

Westo. More than the Spanish in their missions to the south. More than all of these together."

Asha-po rose from his haunches. Thoughtfully he walked across the clearing to the tree that held his knife. He released it with a tug and turned. "Earth mother is good to feed so many mouths."

I groaned. Further definitions of property rights would have to wait for another day.

# 7

*Seven*

*Summer came. It did not arrive like a summer in* England. There the mists and rains of spring would pause to allow the first roses to bloom. Hardly would my mother have the opportunity to enjoy them in her garden before another dreary week of rain spoiled their petals. Rarely was there the feeling that one would ever be warm enough. This was not a problem in Carolina.

As May turned into June, it soon became apparent that the problem was how to become *cool* again. The heat of the sun became merciless. Many of the colonists found it necessary to retreat to their tiny huts for a few hours each midday. But the huts in turn became ovens. They had been thrown up quickly, without thought to ventilation. Added to this discomfort were the insects: flies; mosquitoes;

all manner of buzzing, biting miseries. Julia took to draping a thin length of cotton above her head while she rested, dripping with heat sweat. Soon Mother followed suit. Father took note as he began sketching house plans atop the roughly cobbled tabletop.

"Clearly," he remarked to me one evening after our meal, "clearly, one has to take into consideration the unexpectedly tropical nature of Carolina."

"The latitude should have given us a hint," I pointed out.

"Have you been to Aleppo, Peking, or Jerusalem, Christopher?"

"No, sir."

"Neither have I. Obviously there are more problems in Eden than first met the eye."

"Indeed, sir." I leaned past the candle to squint at his plans. "So you are considering a low house. It will be completely unlike our four floors in London."

"There will be as much space, but spread out. Land is not at a premium here." He pointed his quill at the maze of squares and rectangles he'd drawn within the bold outlines. "See . . . the dining room, the parlour, a dancing and music room—"

I snickered. Formal dancing and music in the wilderness. What a fine conceit.

Father chose to continue. "—chambers for you and Julia; my own chamber with a study attached;

your mother's chamber with a dressing room and a little cabinet room for her treasures, just as in London—"

"What treasures?" I interrupted. "You sold nearly everything before leaving. All she has left are her pewter plates and tankards." I glanced at my mother lying stiffly on her cot across from us in the room no larger than her former cabinet. Try as I might to ignore the fact, the truth hit me like a blow. Our emigration had been hardest on her. The fine London lady now displayed roughened hands instead of kid gloves, strode bare-headed to the fields instead of parading on the Strand.

Father refused to follow my glance. Refused to admit the obvious. "There will be new treasures." He resumed. "A chamber where the maids may lie—"

"What maids?"

His eyebrows furrowed in displeasure. "There will be maids as well. Eventually." He lifted his dry quill point from the future rooms to poke at the porchlike appendage he'd drawn around his edifice. "I have been speaking with the Barbadians. They know how to live in heat. A veranda is necessary. And many large windows so air may circulate."

"But the glass, Father. How can we possibly afford importing all that glass from England?"

"We cannot. Until our colony's own glassworks be organized, we must live with shutters. The Barbadians have devised fine louvers that open and close to admit or keep out the elements." He rolled up his plans and pinched out the flame.

"Enough. To bed now. There are few candles to spare."

I hardly noticed the heat, since whenever possible I took to the forests with Asha-po. It was cooler under the great stands of pine, and the thickness of the leafier woods hid streams where we could fish and wade. Here was my Garden of Eden. I made mention of it one lazy afternoon as we lounged by the bank of a stream, keeping watch over our fishing lines.

"Eden?" Asha-po asked. "This is in England?"

"No. Eden is a kind of myth. A very old story. It is the place we believe people began. Long, long ago. God made the first man, the first woman. He gave them a beautiful place with much food." I motioned around us. "Like this."

"This *God*. Who is he?"

I considered for a long moment. "He is the sun father, also the earth mother. All in one person." It was not a definition that would have pleased the clergy of England, but they were well across the ocean where nothing seemed to please them anyway.

Asha-po nodded. "Sewee begin same way. But far away. Very far away."

This was interesting news. "You mean the Sewee have not always lived here on this land?"

He shook his head. "Same like English, Sewee

come from far, far away. In winter, around night fires, Kenato tells story. Passes down story, from grandfather's mouth to us. Grandfather's grandfather's grandfather tells same story. So we know."

I sighed. "We write our stories in books. Hearing them by the winter fire sounds nicer." I got a tug on my line and paused to haul a nice trout from the stream. Adding it to my string, I rebaited the hook with a fat grub and tossed it back into the water. "Did the Sewee come from across the ocean, too?"

"No." Asha-po jiggled his line. He was now at least one fish short of my catch, but for once he didn't seem to be counting. "Come from west, from where sun father sleeps. Far, far. Hunger comes to old world. Very bad hunger. No game. No nuts or seeds to gather. Nothing but cold." He shivered through the heat of the afternoon.

"It was wintertime?"

"No spring, no summer, no . . ." he searched for the word.

"*Autumn*," I supplied. "When the leaves change their colors."

"Yes, harvest time, *autumn*. No autumn. Only cold. Only winter."

A time of only winter. It was hard to believe. Then I remembered my father's maps back in London. They had shown more than just Europe or Africa or India. They had also shown places to the north. Places I had asked my tutor, John Hawkes, about.

"Iceland and Greenland, Christopher," he'd explained. "And the arctic wastes. Queen Elizabeth sent Sir Martin Frobisher on three expeditions to those parts seeking a Northwest Passage to the Spice Islands, yet he found little but constant ice."

Had the Sewee truly come from such a place? "What happened, Asha-po?"

"Chiefs of all clans meet in great council house. Say people must leave homeland. Must find new land with food. People collect, make things for journey—"

"Prepare?"

"Yes," he agreed. "Prepare. Make big shoes for walk on snow. Many moons walk . . . Always night time . . . Then snow gone. Still night time. . . Walk more moons on hard water—"

"*Ice?*"

Asha-po grunted. "Here sometimes hard water, *ice*, in winter. I see. I step on." He was far away, remembering, searching for the words to express his emotion. "I try to feel what this thing is . . . to walk many moons on such coldness. . . . Try to feel such great strength of my people."

My line twitched, but I ignored it. "What happened *next?*"

"Some people weary. Say, no more walk. They stop. My clan walk more. Walk till they find day again . . . Then walk more. Always, always to where sun rises. To where sun father calls. Then—"

My jiggling fishing line distracted him. I had

knotted the loose end around a heavy rock. Now the rock itself heaved as the twitching changed to a frantic tug-of-war. Asha-po bent to haul in my fish, presenting it to me. "When fish offers spirit, Chris-to-pher, hurt his honor not take."

I smiled. "I did not know that a fish could be insulted." I added the wriggling creature to my string and tossed the lot back into the coolness of the stream without fuss. I wanted to hear the rest of the story. Wiping my hands on my breeches and settling onto my mossy seat again, I summed up Asha-po's tale thus far. "So your people, your clan, chose to keep walking toward the rising sun. What came next?"

Asha-po frowned. "*Next*, they see big snake. Black. Very big, most big—"

"Biggest," I offered. "*Huge*."

"Most *huge* snake ever." He spread his arms wide to show its vastness. "Spread over whole land. Sewee feel big fear." He pounded his heart. "Send most brave warriors to learn, maybe fight. Others wait."

"Was it like an alligator?" I asked. "With horrible teeth?"

Asha-po shook his head. "Snake no have teeth. Snake never have teeth. Brave warriors return. Say *not* snake—"

"*What*?" I leaned forward. "What *was* it?"

Asha-po roared in triumph. "It was forest! *Huge*

forest. Trees hiding much game, much food! We send message to people left behind. . . . But ice gone. . . . People gone. Only much water. Sewee feel sorrow for lost people . . . but Sewee happy we live, happy we—"

"—survive," I interjected.

"Yes. *Survive*." Asha-po beat his chest. "Because brave. Earth mother happy with Sewee. She feeds the brave. Strong again, we follow trees, follow game. Follow sun father. Come here." He folded his arms in satisfaction.

I sat back and smiled. "That was a good story. A most excellent story. Almost better than the Garden of Eden. There was a snake in that story, too, but it was a bad snake, not a good one—" I stopped as Asha-po broke his pose to grasp for his knife. "What are you doing?"

"Do not move, Chris-to-pher."

"But—"

"Do not talk."

The knife shot from his hand, whizzed by my body entirely too closely, and landed with a solid thunk behind me.

"Asha-po," I whispered, frozen in place. "May I move now? May I talk?"

Asha-po sprang to his feet. Already he was kneeling behind me. "Yes, move. Forget talk. Come see."

I turned. Not more than a yard to my rear was a

snake—a *huge* snake curled into a mound. Asha-po's knife had driven its head into the earth. Now he pulled the blade, cleaned and resheathed it, and calmly unwound the writing body. Foot after foot of it . . . Seven feet? . . . Eight feet? I gulped. My mouth suddenly went very dry.

"Look." He forced open its jaws to point out nasty fangs. "*Not* teeth. Snake poison. Very bad medicine. One bite, make dead fast."

He reeled up the thick length of reddish skin patterned with white lines in diamond shapes, coming at last to the tail. It was dry and segmented. He shook it. We listened to the rattle.

"Very bad." He shook it again. "Snake with bad spirit. Earth mother not happy with this snake. She make snake wear noisy tail to warn people. You hear, move quick."

"But we did not hear its rattle," I protested, feeling as if the earth mother had let us down.

"Too busy telling stories. Earth mother give good lesson. *Always* listen." He coiled the length around his shoulders and waist like a piece of rope, cracking a smile. "But earth mother give one more chance. And gift to *remember*. Good taste. Very good taste. Asha-po mother have happy cook pot tonight!"

I stared at the creature in fascination, then felt a curious prickling on my bare arms. Glancing down I saw that my skin had erupted in bumps. Asha-po touched me and pointed toward the stream.

"The fish." My voice cracked over the words.

It was time to collect our bounty and return home. I trailed after Asha-po, unable to tear my eyes from the tail that rattled with sinister glee at his every step. It seemed there were still serpents in the Garden of Eden.

*Eight*

"*Zoons.*"

I had difficulty shaking off my close encounter with the earth mother's bad snake. Her *rattlesnake*. Fish in hand, I stood at the edge of the forest, blending into the very trees the way the Sewee had on that first morning three long months ago. Yet even after tasting the danger of Asha-po's world, I had little heart to join the civilized enclave I spied below.

*Civilized.*

The palisade was complete—guns poking from five ports. Within its walls was the arsenal. There lay our shot and powder in barrels. There hung the colony's twelve suits of armor. I swiped at my brow. Heavy suits of armor in such heat? To wear marching through such wilderness? A half-naked Indian could dance circles around such a European folly. A swift Sewee or Westo arrow could broach its defenses effortlessly. The space that armor had taken in the *Caroline*'s holds could have been better used packed with my mother's lost treasures of painted china and finely polished furniture—or with my sister Julia's harpsichord. Then there would have been something to fill all those rooms my father planned to build . . . something to give my mother hope during her days of drudgery.

I turned to the fields—the fields of my mother and the other women. The corn was growing, spreading its arms to heaven. I smiled. Mother must have said her prayers. Yet little else flourished—

"*Oof*!"

*Always listen*, Asha-po had warned. Not listening, I was nearly bowled over from behind. I jerked around to face my assailant: a huge, broad-snouted *pig*. It lunged at my fish.

"A pox upon all pigs!"

I snatched my bounty from the very maw of the fat sow, aimed and landed a solid kick on her heaving side.

"*Pigs!*" I spat.

There were pigs everywhere. Of all our livestock, they alone thrived mightily. And why not? Pigs were given the liberty of the woods each morning. After rooting happily all day, they rushed home

to another meal each evening at the call of a horn. I
gave the insolent creature another clout, but it was
hardly necessary. Standing next to his master's fence
below me, Burnaby Bull raised a horn to his lips and
blew. The sow pricked up her ears and waddled off
with a grunt of pleasure.

"Good riddance," I muttered after it.

"Christopher? Who are you talking to?"

I spun. "Julia! You crept up on me like an Indian!"

My sister grinned. "I've been practicing.
Sneaking into the woods when Father isn't watching. This afternoon was an especially good
opportunity because Mother retired, feeling poorly
again, and Father went off reconnoitering in the
sloop with that surveyor, Mr. Culpepper. I really
think I don't like Mr. Culpepper. Something about
the set of his eyes . . ."

She spotted my string at last. "*Ooh*. More lovely
fish. May I take them home? They're sure to cheer
Mother since they are the easiest possible meal to
cook—if *you* clean them."

I handed her the string. "A skill it is time to pass
on to you, my dear sister."

"Scaling? Gutting?" Her enthusiasm dimmed.
"Honestly, Christopher. I grow so *weary* of this
place. All I end up with is the dead fish. I want to see
where they're caught, what they're like alive. Please
take me with you one day! I want to see the Indian

village, too. I want to know what the Indian girls are doing. I want—"

I grabbed her blond braid and gave it a playful tug to stop her chatter. "They are doing exactly what you and Mother and the other colonists of the gentler sex are doing. Tending the gardens. Preparing the meals."

Julia swung the fish at me. I ducked.

"*Female*. That's all I am. How I wish I could be a boy like you. If I were a boy, Father couldn't hold me down. I *am* old enough. I was twelve my last birthday! I could go exploring, I could—"

"Give me the fish before you do our supper harm." I reached for the string. "You didn't mind being a girl in London, did you? You got to play at watercolors and music and fine stitchery while I was stuck with Latin and philosophy lessons."

"A fine lot of good any of that did either of us," Julia shot back. "It were better if we had had lessons in carpentry, or brick making, or something useful like the servants learn."

"Julia!" I caught her shoulders and gave her a fishy hug. "Julia! You're growing up!"

She stuck out her tongue in a very immature fashion and raced off toward the shore where our father was hauling the colony's sole boat from the water. I studied the sloop, then the single sail Mr. Culpepper was struggling to make fast. Here lay another misconception of the Lord Proprietors: a boat neither large enough to return us to England, nor small enough to slip inland through the passages of the marshlands. It would be far better to make canoes like the Sewee . . . I sighed. Carolina colonists would never do anything so *un*civilized.

Pausing to *listen* to the forest surrounding me, I stepped from its embrace into my other world.

"Fish again?"

That was the extent of Father's grace over the evening meal. I wondered what his reaction would have been to rattlesnake.

"Is there no meat to be had?" His complaint continued. Obviously his voyage in the sloop had not been entirely satisfactory.

"The Sewee say we must allow the deer to mature over the summer, Father," I replied. "After their mating season in the autumn we may hunt again, but only the bucks. In the meantime I've been taking beavers and muskrats in the traps. Stephen Fox, the tanner, says they will make fine pelts for the next ship, although winter pelts would be even richer. He says—"

Father crinkled his nose. "Enough of Stephen Fox. One would almost believe oneself to be back in London with the smells that have been issuing from his tannery works."

"Maybe you could ask him to move the works off a bit, Father," I suggested. "To the edge of the settlement."

"The pigs, too," Julia piped up. "And the cattle. They bring the flies—"

"I have no authority over where a man chooses to keep his household or his business," Father pointed out. "Not unless by doing so he endangers the safety of the rest of us."

"But the smells . . . the insects." Mother quietly added her thoughts. She did look pale beneath her bleached hair and the sunburn of her face. "Surely these can be a danger. . ."

"That will all be behind us when we take our own lands. The present danger is a far different one."

"What?" Julia and I cried out.

Father glared at his plate of fish, then at us, as if we were all part and parcel of his current dilemma. Finally he shoved his plate away.

"Truth be told, your trout is fine, Christopher. But I have no stomach for it at the moment." He studied the tender, pale flesh he had rejected. "Such fish, so fresh, could be enjoyed in England only by the likes of Lord Ashley. Could only be taken from his private streams." He glanced at me. "You do remember the meals at Ashley's estate, Christopher?"

"Yes, sir," I nodded. "He served his trout with dilled butter and a dry, white French wine. If Mother's dill seeds prosper we could enjoy the same this time next year. I cannot guarantee you the wine, though."

Father actually cracked a smile. "A fine, dry wine is the least of my worries at the moment."

Mother, Julia, and I forsook our own suppers to stare at him. Would he go the next step? Would he choose to share his worry with us, his family? We watched Father think long and hard. We watched him reach for his tankard and raise it to his lips. He spat out a mouthful. "Water."

"The ale barrels went dry, Joseph," Mother apologized. "But the spring water here is so unlike that of the water in London as to be quite healthful—"

"*Water!*" Father raised his tankard again, this time to make a toast. "To the Colony of Carolina! May she prosper through water and treason!"

"*Treason!*" We gasped the word as one.

"You will be hearing soon enough." Father set down his tankard. "Gossip flows faster through this settlement than our vanished ale once did. That treacherous villain Brian Fitzpatrick—"

"Mr. Culpepper's indentured servant?" Julia asked.

"The same."

Father's displeasure was fearful to behold. I thanked heaven that for once it was not directed toward me.

"He's absconded. Last seen headed south toward the Spanish colony. That's why Culpepper and I took out the sloop today. We ran some miles along the coast, thinking Fitzpatrick had not the guts to take to the forest."

"You found no sign of him?" I asked.

"Nothing. He was heard making complaints that five years of indenture was too heavy a price for a few acres of sandy land." Father ran a hand through his dark hair. A few streaks of silver shone in it. New streaks. "Too heavy a price. Too much work. Now he is off to announce our colony to the Spanish, who had no inkling of our presence up to this point—and he takes one of our precious flintlocks with him."

"One of our flintlocks!" I cried. Brian Fitzpatrick was a villain indeed. That was a weapon I could have grown into. Though seething with the unfairness of it all, I tried to consider the positive side. "It will take him weeks to make his way to Saint Augustine on foot, Father." I pictured the journey in my mind, knowing now what I did of the wilderness. "And if he did take to the forests or swamps, there are dangerous creatures to stop him. Alligators. Rattlesnakes—"

"The ungodly who make such pacts with the devil usually survive, Christopher."

"Perhaps . . ." Another thought entered my mind, one worse than that rascal Fitzpatrick's treachery. "Er . . . should he really find his way to St. Augustine where the Spanish authorities live, where they keep their ships . . . how long would it take them to sail north? To Carolina?"

Father's answer came too quickly. "They will wait for the prevailing southeast wind. With such a wind, the Spanish could be at our backs in three days."

Mother's handkerchief suddenly appeared between her fingers. She began the wringing motion I had not seen for some time. "What must we do, husband?"

Father rose from the table. He had worked out his anger and was sure of himself again. "I must call another assembly. Guards must be posted. Our colony must be put on full alert. Immediately."

Nine

Mr. Florence O'Sullivan was a bachelor. Since he had no family to protect, he was unanimously elected to be the new—and first—resident of a small island some miles off the shore of our colony near the entrance to our bay. Here he was to set up a lookout for the Spanish fleet.

"But it be bone dry!" he spluttered. "With hardly a tree for shelter!"

From my seat astride a driftwood log at the edge of that night's proceedings, I watched my father nearly skewer the poor soul with his fierce look. "While sailing past its shores in the sloop with Mr. Culpepper, I counted at least three palms."

"*Civilized* trees, I'm meaning!"

"The needs of the entire colony must be met, Mr. O'Sullivan. Yours will be the most important post. You will be in a position to spy enemy traffic first, then give warning to those ashore."

"But . . ."

Mr. O'Sullivan's protests were in vain. At first light the next morning the sloop was filled with water barrels, provisions, and a selection of weathered canvas for shelter. Before noon Mr. O'Sullivan warily took his place next to the small gun and balls removed from the palisade port confronting the forest. Immediate danger was expected from the sea, after all. Should it come, O'Sullivan was to set off a warning shot to notify those ashore. Glumly he allowed himself to be ferried to the isolated island to begin his sentry duties.

Alas, this present alarm was to change my status, too. All able-bodied men were now set on guard duty. For the most part they were allowed to proceed with their usual chores—always keeping an eye to the horizon and a weapon at hand. Not quite a man, yet older by far than the colony's other boys, I no longer had the luxury of being torn between civilization and the wilderness. Father put a stop to my escapes into the forest. Yet he still expected me to feed our family. More to the point, I had to feed a good portion of the colonists as well, now that the other hunters must also keep close to the settlement.

Unable to meet Asha-po at our lone palm that

dawn, I chose a propitious moment to slip away one last time into the trees. I found my friend by the bank of our favorite stream.

"Chris-to-pher. What happens in village? English like bees smoked from hive."

"A Spanish scare."

I knelt down and explained the larger issue. Then I presented my own particular problem.

He listened gravely to everything. He considered. At last he nodded. "English village need food. Chris-to-pher must not leave village."

"At least not go into the forest."

He nodded again. "Asha-po show you other food. Food waiting in sand, waiting in Great Water. Take trouble from mind, from heart. Earth mother hide food everywhere. Sewee learn to look. Chris-to-pher learn to look, to find."

Thus began my apprenticeship as a clam digger.

The urchins of London regularly worked the tidal flats of the River Thames. On errands around the city, I'd often paused to watch them rake for cockles and mussels and the occasional clam. In fine weather it seemed a wonderful pastime. Skirts were tucked into waistbands and breeches tugged above knees in a rare show of liberty, as the children tramped along hard sands and waded into the muck. I longed to frolic with them, even though the waters be filthy.

In weather less fine I had watched the same bare legs turn blue and hugged my warm clothing to my body in thanksgiving. Later I might spare a ha'penny to taste their hard-won bounty as they hawked it through the streets. What those urchins wouldn't give to trade places with me now; to rake fine, juicy clams from shining sands next to pristine waters.

I straightened from the clam bed I had been working to ease my back. "I should have paid them more. They deserved more than a ha'penny. This is hard labor!"

Asha-po turned from where he'd been staring out to sea. "You speak, Chris-to-pher?"

I leaned into the rake. "It was nothing. I was only remembering England."

"Ah. England." He glanced at the progress I'd made, then walked over to reach for the rake. Upending it he examined each tine. "Hard," he declared. "It work better than stick."

"Iron," I explained. "It's made of iron, like the hoes and the axes."

"Hoes English women use in fields, yes?"

"Yes."

"Better for corn than stick, too." He set down the rake and gave it a few swipes through the sand. "My mother like hoe, like rake. Save much work." He looked at me. "My father—Asha-po, too—like ax. More sharp than stone hatchet. Save much work."

I knelt down to pull a clam from the trove I'd uncovered. The liquid sand around it *shlurshed* and slowly crept back to refill the void.

"Hand me my knife, Asha-po."

He tossed it from next to the waiting barrel already half-full with the evening's meal. I carefully split the clam open and offered it to him, then reached for another for myself. The juice was sweet and tangy and the clam refreshing as it slid down my throat. I cleaned the knife blade in the sand, then held it up.

"This blade is made of *steel*, Asha-po, just like your knife. It's a kind of *iron*, but finer than what we use to make rakes and hoes and axes. Your mother *would* like a hoe. Your father *would* like an ax. You *would* like an ax, too." I paused in my grammar lesson to look at my friend. "I *would* like to give you all of these things. But I cannot. The big ships did not bring enough for trade. They only brought enough for the English to use."

Asha-po grunted and swerved toward the endless horizon again. "I *would* like to know when big ships return. I *would* like big ships to carry many hoes, many axes."

"I would like that, too. All of that." With a sigh, I began harvesting more clams.

We ate clams raw. We ate clams in broth. We ate clams steamed for hours, Sewee-style, in damp piles of seaweed beneath the coals of our fires. When even I had eaten enough clams to last a lifetime, I turned to Asha-po yet again for help. He had taken to presenting himself for at least part of my work days. Others did, too. My sister Julia and her friends crept along the sands within sight of my struggles and giggled, then disappeared without offers of aid. But Asha-po was different.

"I believe it is time to thank the earth mother for her wonderful clams." I gave the rake a rest and broached the subject foremost in my mind. I did so as tactfully as possible. "A good way to thank her might be to allow them to grow into their bounty once more—the way the deer grow to fullness before mating season."

"Ah."

He assessed the length of beach I'd worked over. I studied it with him. Already I had progressed a good mile past the edges of the settlement. I had no doubt that I could continue in that direction all the way to Florida and the Spanish, harvesting a bounty of clams the entire way. That accomplished, I could return and begin working my way north.

Maybe a similar thought occurred to Asha-po, because he smiled. "English like many tastes in mouths. Full stomach not enough."

I shrugged my shoulders and grinned. "You understand better than I had hoped."

"Rattlesnake make happy cook pot, too, after

many days of meal. Sewee like many tastes, too. But my people, they . . ."

I watched him reach for another word. "Satisfied?" I asked. "The Sewee are satisfied—"

"Yes, Sewee *satisfied* with only full stomach."

"You are satisfied with enough." I sighed. "I fear we English must learn to be satisfied with enough very soon now, too. But in the meantime . . ."

Asha-po considered the meantime. "Corn on ears grows, but not big, not soft."

"No," I agreed.

"English have no hard corn from last harvest to make meal."

"No," I agreed again. More to the point, our flour barrels were emptying at an alarming rate. Water could be substituted for ale, but what could be substituted for bread?

My worried frown must have upset my friend. He touched my arm. "For now, find more clams. Tomorrow morning, meet at tree."

"Our tree? Will you bring your canoe?" I asked. I did miss our dawn excursions.

Asha-po agreed. "Chris-to-pher rest troubled spirit. Still guard land from Spanish. But guard land from water, not from sand. Find new tastes for English mouths!"

Asha-po's new tastes were amazing indeed. And the hunting was even more amazing. Shortly after dawn on the morrow, we anchored the canoe a distance offshore. Asha-po slipped over the side, made a show of taking a huge breath of air—and, holding it within his lungs, disappeared into the depths. I watched the bubbles rise and waited for his head to rise with them. It did not. He was gone a long time. He was gone so long that I had leisure to consider a new thought. Should he ever rise again, Asha-po expected me to do likewise. He actually expected me to immerse myself in the *sea*. In the *deep* sea. I clutched at the sides of the canoe in terror.

It's not that I minded bathing. I had gone to bathhouses in London several times a year, always keeping in mind John Hawkes's admonition to let the moon be in Libra or Pisces. But I'd neglected to check the moon lately, and this might not be an auspicious moment. . . . I had even washed my feet fairly regularly without undo rash exposure to colds—something I hadn't had to trouble myself with in Carolina since I'd forsaken my boots. But to plunge myself entire into the depths of the ocean—

"**Hah!**" Asha-po popped up at last.

"You're not drowned!"

He grasped for the canoe with one hand and drank in long drafts of air. His lungs at ease again, Asha-po raised his submerged hand, brandishing in it an *immense*, villainous-looking creature. "Have care, Chris-to-pher."

That was all. Only, "Have care, Christopher," and suddenly I was sharing the canoe with a shifty-eyed monster on the attack with lethal, snapping claws. I backed away fast, but not before one of those claws seized the hem of my breeches and cut through it like a knife to butter.

"*Zoons!*"

Asha-po shoved his head over the side of the canoe, tipping it precariously. "You like?"

I continued edging toward the stern of the canoe with all speed. The monster scuttled forward in angry pursuit. "I . . . I . . . I think it's a *lobster*. But England *never* had such a lobster! Those claws! They must weigh five pounds each!"

Asha-po was grinning, pleased with himself. "Much meat in hands, in *claws*. Feed many English."

My spine banged into the stern. I could retreat no farther.

Asha-po was enjoying my dilemma, but finally let up. "We tie claws, make safe."

"Good." I breathed again, but my relief came too soon.

"After *you* find one."

"*Me?*"

His grin broadened. "You."

I studied the enraged lobster before me, then the swells of the water around me. Caught between two devils. I gulped. "I am afraid, afraid that—" I swallowed again and made my confession like a man. "I don't know how to swim, Asha-po."

"*Swim?*"

I jerked my head toward the sea. "In water. I don't know how to move in water. To swim." I fear my lament came out as more of a wail than I had intended. Not at all manlike. I proclaimed the obvious once more. "I *cannot* swim!"

Asha-po laughed. He absolutely roared. In the midst of a fresh bellow of mirth, he reached up to loosen my fingers' death grip on the sides of his canoe. Without further ado he flipped me into the water. As I sank below the surface, the last words I ever expected to hear reached my ears:

"We fix fast."

## Ten

*I created quite a stir lugging eighty pounds of* lobster into the settlement that afternoon. My swimming lessons had been direct and to the point. Learn or drown. I learned. Yet the learning took much of the day, and even with my bounty—and the equal number of lobsters my friend hauled to his own village—Asha-po was not satisfied.

"Tomorrow we do better, Chris-to-pher."

I studied the gashes on my arms—even on my legs. I had discovered fast enough that one does not master swimming in one's waterlogged breeches. Neither does one capture lobsters without a battle.

"Tomorrow we bring more vines to bind the claws together quickly, very quickly," I answered.

Since my father grew daily more irascible as the traitor Brian Fitzpatrick's absence lengthened, I should have anticipated his reaction at the evening meal.

"Having survived a month's penance with clams, am I now to expect a month of lobster? *Fish, clams, lobster*," he groused. "I begin to feel like a papist, and it be neither Friday nor Lent."

Mother rubbed her temples. "The air is too heavy for dissent at table this evening, husband. It seems to have been building all the afternoon. Never was there such heaviness in the English climate." She continued the massaging motion. It did not seem to ease the weariness in her face, nor stiffen the slump of her shoulders. "Instead of discord, we should be seeking harmony. We should be thanking God for the abundance He has laid into Christopher's hands."

I glanced at my hands, then at my bare arms beneath the rolled sleeves of the linen shirt Mother required me to don for meals. Had God been responsible as well for the scars I would surely be left with? If so, we needed to come to some understanding on the subject of lobsters.

"I like it," Julia declared. "It's delicious, and I think I could eat lobster forever." She attacked her portion of tail with relish. "And all you have to do is throw it into boiling water until it turns red."

That made me smile. Julia's definition of a good dinner was always one that required the least amount of effort to prepare.

"But—" she swallowed, "—I don't understand why I cannot be allowed to learn to swim so I might help Christopher dive for lobsters, too—"

"No!" Father yelped. "Never! I will not have my only daughter marring her fine skin!"

So he *had* noticed my mementos. I opened my mouth to say a few words in Julia's favor, but she overtook me. Perhaps the climate was affecting her temperament as well.

"I am *not* to go into the forest," Julia declared. "I am *not* to associate with the Sewee. I am *not* allowed to mar my fine skin!" My sweet little sister glared, positively glared, at our parent. "What, then, am I *allowed* to do, Father?"

His face turned as red as the lobster shell before him. "Recite your catechism!" he finally barked. "At once!"

Mother abandoned massaging her temples to press her forehead as if a great pain lodged within. Beside me, my sister heaved a mighty sigh. At last she lowered her eyes and recited the words we had both grown up with, the words we had been required to repeat every Sunday of our lives at church service in England. They were words we'd had neither the time to consider nor the clergy to oversee in Carolina.

"'My duty toward my neighbor is to love him as myself, and to do to all men as I would they should do unto me—'" Julia whispered.

"Less reticence, if you please," Father commanded. "With as much force of enthusiasm as your former words."

"'—to love, honor and succor my father and mother,'" she plowed on with exaggerated vigor, "'to submit myself to all my governors, teachers, spiritual pastors and masters; to order myself lowly and reverently to all my betters—'"

"That will do," Father interrupted. "And what do those words signify to you, daughter? What does *submit* signify to you?"

Julia's mouth opened, but her answer never got out.

**Craaaack.**

It was the sound of the heavens themselves being rent in twain. Either that, or—

We jumped. All of us.

"O'Sullivan!" Father exclaimed, Julia's catechism lesson forgotten.

"The Spanish?" the rest of us breathed. It had been a word always on our minds, yet rarely spoken—a word building in intensity. Building like the humidity of the evening and my father's temper along with it.

"It has been more than a month since Fitzpatrick absconded . . ." Father voiced his fears aloud at last.

**Booooom.**

We upended our stools in rushing out the door.

The entire colony was of one mind with our family. Everyone had left his evening meal to rush to the shore. Together we watched as livid storm clouds gathered over the sea. Together we spied a tremendous flash of lightning break above the growing waves. Together we heard the next *boom*. Cannons or the upheaval of nature? Or both? Surely there had never been such thunder sounding over London.

Heads swung toward Father. He it was who must explain, interpret, calm. I suddenly knew it to be a burden heavier than the storm bearing down on us. The knowledge made it easier to forgive his recent choler.

Father spread his arms as if in prayer—or supplication. "It cannot be known," he shouted above the rising wind. "Mayhap the cannon sounded."

The wind increased. Lightning flashed again, closer. Heavy rain began to fall.

"Yet . . . perhaps 'tis only a storm."

The rain turned drenching, a force in itself.

"Look to your protection—" Father's voice fought through the deluge, "—be it from the heavens or the Spanish!"

It was enough. I caught my mother as she staggered from the onslaught and led her back to our hut. There we four stood with protective arms about each other while the sky blackened in fury, while the wind and rain tore at our frail walls. I glanced at the roof above us. It was newly thatched the way Asha-po had recommended. As the elements battled, I prayed the wisdom of the Sewee might see us through yet again.

Morning brought a scene of devastation. Half the dwellings of the settlement had not withstood the fury of the storm. Only those with thatched roofs remained. I wandered among the dazed colonists, then down to the shore. There I found something—someone—I had not expected.

"Mr. O'Sullivan!"

For it was, indeed, Florence O'Sullivan slumped on the sand, looking much the worse for wear than when we'd sent him off to exile a month back.

"What are you doing here? *How* did you get here? Are the Spanish really coming? Are—"

He bestirred himself to halt my questions with a raised hand. "No Spanish. No Spanish did I see the entire time. And no Spanish do I ever expect to see. What interest could they possibly have in our pitiful endeavors? No," he continued, warming to his words, as if he had waited an entire month to let them be heard. "Not a soul did I speak to for over thirty days and thirty nights. Not a soul did I see, save the heathens—"

"The Sewee?" I broke in. "The Sewee came to visit you?"

"In their canoes. They paddled silently past my beach on occasion. They even left me a fish now and again, seeing I was nigh on perishing from hunger. When they turned up again this dawn—methinks to learn if I survived the storm—I had had enough."

He glared at me ferociously, as if I had taken exception to his tale. Far from it. My nod of sympathy set him off again.

"Had not the tempest destroyed what little shelter I'd fashioned for myself? Had not I spent the night unprotected under its deluge? Duty or not, a man must reach his limit. Last night was mine. Come the sun, I waded out to the nearest canoe and let myself in. And here they delivered me."

He struggled to his knees at last. "Thirty days and thirty nights, lad. Alone with myself. Even the rightful wrath of Joseph West cannot make me return."

I held out my hand. "Best get the news over with the soonest then, sir."

Florence O'Sullivan accepted my aid and stumbled after me to his fate.


"You abandoned your post! You abandoned the Colony of Carolina's gun!"

I expected Father in his high dudgeon to be shouting his disapproval to the entire colony. Yet even in his righteous anger he had moderated the volume of his discourse. He was furious, yes, but I found I needed to creep close to our hut to follow his seething words.

Now safely upon the mainland once more, Florence O'Sullivan remained unrepentant. "*You* spend thirty days and thirty nights alone upon that desolate isle, Joseph West. *You* spend 'em with the pitiful supply of provisions that were sent with me. *Then* may you judge. Before God Almighty, I did my best, until I could do so no longer."

There was a pause. I wished I could see my father's face to read it. He spoke at last. His words came with a great weariness.

"You speak some truth, O'Sullivan, yet rules of the colony require that I make report to the Lord Proprietors of your seditious act—"

"Seditious act!" Mr. O'Sullivan blustered. "How can escaping from that barren desert before perishing be construed a seditious act?"

"It was resistance to the lawful authority of the Colony of Carolina. You were a soldier and you deserted your post in our time of need. You did not consider your role as submissive to the needs of the greater group. I regret it, Florence—"

There it was, *submission* again. Julia and I and our mother to Father. Mr. O'Sullivan to the colony and its head, Father again. Was there no place upon this great Earth where a person could stand tall without submitting?

"—but I am compelled to secure your colony land against your future good behavior. For the rest, we must wait for another ship to send the complaint."

"Much good my future acres lying fallow will do anyone." Mr. O'Sullivan sniffed. "'Twill be a cold day in hell before you find another fool to set foot on that wretched isle to await the coming of your Spanish."

I didn't bother listening to the conclusion of the affair. I sped off in search of Asha-po. If I could not have the wilderness, might I not have a desert isle instead? There—at least for a little while—I need submit to no man save myself. To boot, there could be a chance at battle with the Spanish!

## Eleven

*I waited till Father had finished haranguing* the colonists at the evening's emergency assembly. There were no volunteers for sentry duty.

"Be cast away upon O'Sullivan's island? Not I!"

"Nor I!"

"It's a medallion we should be casting for the man, not shunning him," Samuel Bull proclaimed.

The shouts slowed to grumbles and murmurs. I stood up.

"The meeting has not yet adjourned, Christopher West," Father barked.

"I wasn't leaving, sir. I was about to request permission to speak."

He studied me a long moment. "Granted."

I took a deep breath, as deep as if I were about to dive into the depths of the sea, which perhaps I was.

"And yet, honored gentlemen," I began, "and yet the Spanish still may come upon their southeast wind."

I ignored the glares from the men around me. The central fire gave little illumination, but I could feel in full the displeasure of Samuel Bull and Mr. Culpepper and even Dr. Henry Woodward—himself a bachelor like O'Sullivan. Steadfastly I soldiered on. "Keeping that in mind, I wish to volunteer myself for sentry duty on the island." I smiled. "On Mr. O'Sullivan's Island."

Silence.

Father at last cut through it. "Thank you, son. The Colony of Carolina appreciates your generous offer. Unfortunately, you be too young to take on the responsibility—"

"Too young?" My voice almost broke, but I caught it in time. "With all due respect, sir, am I also then too young to supply daily food for our company? I will attain my sixteenth year in the next month—"

Voices were stirring again in the darkness under the stars.

"The lad, er, the *young man* has a point."

"And speaks well for his age."

"And has done a mighty job of provisioning—"

"Exactly!" my father broke in. "And who shall provision us in his absence?"

I spoke again, more quickly. "The others in their

minority, sir. While there is a dearth of young men,
there is none of young ladies: my sister and the other
young women. They have been studying my clamming methods and are quite capable of taking up the
task from me."

"*Clams* . . ." floated like a sigh through the gathering.

"It is not dangerous work," I swiftly added. "It
can be done within sight of the colony itself. Nor is
it difficult. One needs but a low tide and an eye for
the breathing holes." I paused a brief moment for
the idea to catch hold. Then, before too much thinking could be done, "If allowed, I would be bold to
make one further suggestion."

I waited as Father shook his head.

"Proceed," he said with reluctance.

I nodded deferentially and offered the final ele-
ment of my carefully planned strategy. "Mr.
O'Sullivan remained at his post for thirty days. Allow
me to take it up from him for but half that period—
a fortnight. At the conclusion of that time perhaps
another volunteer might be forthcoming. If there is a
limit to the duty, the task will not be as onerous."

"Wisely spoken!"

"As one beyond his years!"

"The young man is a credit to you, West!"

What could my father say? I had snared him as
sweetly as in a Sewee trap.

Father shrugged in defeat. "Does the company so vote?" he finally asked.

Ayes of relief filled the night.

"So be it." My father turned to me. "The sloop will be provisioned at dawn. Hold yourself in readiness."

"Yes, sir. Thank you, sir."

The women of our household had even less enthusiasm for my new task than my father.

"You volunteered me to dig clams?" Julia wailed. "How *could* you, Christopher!"

"Almost sixteen though he be," Mother began, "Christopher is not yet a man, Joseph! I have held my tongue in wifely submission while he disappeared into the wilderness, held it while he scarred himself for life with those lobsters. I cannot hold it longer." She faced my father squarely, blue eyes blazing. "He is our only remaining son and your heir, yet you send him into danger beyond our ken!"

Father sat by the table looking harassed. I grabbed my mother and hugged her. "There is nothing to burn upon that island, Mother. No plague awaits me there."

"But still—"

Father stopped any further protest. "The idea was your son's, Elizabeth, not mine. What's done is done, and we must live with the decision."

Joseph West had spoken. For once I was glad of it.

This time around I took a much greater interest in the provisions stowed within the sloop. Along with the water barrels and such dried victuals as were at hand—chiefly moldering ship biscuit, I fear to say—I also requested and received tools, nails, additional cannonballs and gunpowder. Father balked, however, at my request for a flintlock.

"No."

"But if the Spanish come—"

"If the Spanish come they will never get within shooting distance of a flintlock. If the Spanish come you have my permission to fire balls at them to your heart's content."

"But if I need to hunt—"

"Hunt what? O'Sullivan has sworn to the barrenness of the isle. Should the man have exaggerated, you have your heathen weapons at hand. They seem to have stood you in good stead until now."

"But . . ."

Father stared down my protest. "I require every flintlock for defense of the colony on the mainland, Christopher. You know this, yet you still challenge me? Consider well. Need I ask *you* to recite your catechism?"

"Submission of the lowest to the highest, for the

good of the greater number," I mumbled. Father caught my words but chose not to comment further. It was time for the leave-taking.

I boarded the sloop, along with Mr. Godfrey, who'd taken to calling himself *Colonel*, and Dr. Woodward. Whether Godfrey had true military experience or not, he was my father's chosen assistant for security affairs within the colony. His current task was to set himself upon the island long enough to instruct me on usage of the gun lying in wait. Father stood by the prow, ready to shove the boat fully into the water. He shifted his shoulders to the task—

"Wait!"

The cry halted us. I had expected nothing in the way of a grand sendoff. All hands in the colony were set to repairing storm damage. Yet a glance back revealed my sister scrambling down the shore. She huffed up beside the hull and stretched to hand me something.

I grabbed her offering. "Julia! It's your hare's foot from England!"

"Wear it round your neck, Christopher, with your shells. It will keep you from colic, and toothache, and . . ."

Her silliness was kind, and it warmed me. "Thank you, little sister."

"Oh." She reached within her skirts for another

gift—a large twist of our precious salt. "Mother worries over your teeth, too. She says remember to clean them with this each night."

"The tide turns!" Father heaved at the sloop.

Julia ran alongside as it splashed into the water. "And I don't really mind clamming, Christopher. It will be a change from gardening, although lobstering would be so much more fun. . . ."

Dr. Woodward unfurled the sail and we were off. I waved my farewells and turned to the sea.

Twelve

*The voyage was nine or ten miles by sea.* We were driven north before fair winds—prevailing southeast winds—which fact I forbore mentioning to my companions. What purpose in adding to their unease? Neither of them seemed to have a taste for the water, and I knew for a certainty that Colonel Godfrey had not spent the crossing from England mingling with and learning the lore of sailors as I had. Colonel Godfrey had spent it abed, greener than the waves we rode upon. When O'Sullivan's Island bore into view, Godfrey took in the sight with relief.

"Right, then. Off you go, lad."

It was unnecessary to give answer to the man. We were still a quarter mile from the shore. But eventually the sloop was beached on a ledge of hard sand. My provisions were unloaded in a hasty pile, and I was given hastier lessons in the use of the three-pounder which Florence O'Sullivan had abandoned half-sunk in the dunes. Then the sloop was away with such dispatch that one would have thought the isle to be haunted. I smiled as the sail disappeared to the south, then laughed aloud as Asha-po's canoe hove into view from the north. The joys of sentry duty stretched before me.

"What is *desert*, Chris-to-pher?" Asha-po asked that evening as we turned freshly caught fish over the embers of our small fire.

I pulled my fish from the heat and tested it. It flaked nicely. Done to a turn. It was good, but could be improved. I reached into my pocket for Mother's twist of salt. There were better uses for it than teeth scouring. I scattered a precious pinch over the skewered flesh, then passed the salt to Asha-po.

"*Desert* means a hard place, Asha-po. A place without life, without food. And especially without water."

He carefully retwisted the salt and returned it, then kept his silence for several long minutes as we devoured our supper. At last, with a soft belch of satisfaction, he lay back on the sand to stare at the rising moon.

"Why English call this island *desert*?" he inquired at last. "Much food here. Even water here—"

"If you know where to look," I answered. "Most English . . ." I shook my head. "Unfortunately, most English have not the patience for the looking." I cleaned my hands with a fistful of sand and eased myself down to stare at the stars twinkling into life.

"This *patience*," Asha-po murmured. "I think patience most English never have."

I made a Seweelike grunt and rolled into my blanket.

With the dawn we began our explorations. First we paced the length of the isle, some three miles. When the sun reached its meridian we paused beneath the shade of a palm to make our noon meal from the trove of clams we'd unearthed within yards of our resting place. Thus refreshed, Asha-po and I set off inland. Once past the line of hard, white beach along the coast and the rise of dunes above, we encountered a dense undergrowth of a bushy shrub. I plucked one of the shiny, dark green, lance-shaped leaves akin to English laurel and called by some *myrtle*. Absently, I crushed it between my fingers. An exotic aroma enveloped me.

"The smell!" I exclaimed. "This is the fragrance that overtook me last night when the wind shifted."

Asha-po smiled. "Good for night visions."

"Dreams?"

"If spirit calm, this make more calm. If spirit not

calm, make bad vision, bad dream. Flowers gone
now—" he pointed at the dried remains of one, "—but
when many, many flowers, smell very strong."

"Poor Mr. O'Sullivan." I studied the acres and
acres of laurel spread before us. "With his excitable
nature and these flowers all in full bloom, it's a
wonder he lasted thirty days upon this isle."

Having little interest in the well-being of someone as incompetent as Florence O'Sullivan, Asha-po
merely wielded the English ax I had lent him and
began cutting through the shoulder-high barrier,
and I followed in the path he hewed. Soon the plants
expanded in wild abandon—higher than our heads—
and our path became a tunnel. We took turns
carving our way through this denser growth. After
struggling for nearly a quarter of a mile, Asha-po
stopped quite suddenly, and I crashed into him.

"What is it?"

"Sssh," he hissed. "Food."

I peeked over his shoulder. We'd come to the
end of the myrtle jungle. In fact, we had come to the
end of O'Sullivan's Island. Ahead was the mainland,
unmistakable in its own dense growth of cedar and
cyprus. But in between—in between was a broad
creek oozing its way through reeds. And nearly at
Asha-po's feet was—

He swooped down and plucked the marsh hen
from her nest. One swift, wringing motion was all it

took to painlessly wrench the creature's neck. In a moment she was lodging in the game bag slung from his shoulders. In another, he was sucking at one of the eggs nestled in their bed of soft grasses. He swallowed and grinned.

"Hen sits late on eggs. Bad for hen. Good for us." Asha-po nodded for me to join him.

I bent to reach for one of the eggs. "The usual English custom is to cook one's eggs before eating them."

I held the small orb in hand, hesitating. How long since I had eaten a fresh egg? Some of the colonists had brought English hens with them, but being a City man, Father hadn't thought that far ahead. And an egg was a grace one rarely shared with the neighbors. I hesitated still, while Asha-po consumed the remainder of his share.

"Chris-to-pher not like eggs?"

"Christopher loves eggs. *Cooked* eggs."

Asha-po waved at the marsh facing us. "No fire here. Carry egg to camp, egg break. Then no egg. Gift of earth mother wasted."

I sighed. It would not do to insult the earth mother. I nicked the top of the egg with my knife and squeezed the contents into my mouth. And gagged. And spat.

"*What in heaven's name*—"

"Little bird ready to come out."

Asha-po shook his head in pity. For me or the bird? I pointed at the remaining egg. "It's all yours, Asha-po."

Asha-po was so full of energy after his egg feast that he insisted we muck about in the slime on our side of the creek. Herons and egrets took to brief flight, then cautiously returned to their fishing chores within yards of us. Woodpeckers from clear across the creek let out their high bright calls:

*kent! . . . kent! . . . kent!*

They were like the blaring notes of brass horns to the egrets' flutes. My head fair burst with listening to the orchestra around me. There were more subtle musicians, too: water snakes swishing between our bare legs, rock-basking turtles poking their heads from beneath their shells with near-soundless pops.

To such accompaniment we set trap after trap, till even I wondered if the two of us could eat the bounty that was sure to greet us on the morrow. At last, with the sun beginning its descent in the west, we scrambled back through our myrtle tunnel. The sand and sea still awaited us. I blinked back the dazzling vision, then slammed my head with my fist.

"Fool! Idiot!"

"What, Chris-to-pher?"

"The Spanish, Asha-po. I forgot to keep watch for the Spanish the entire afternoon!"

He pointed south. "Look now. No big ships."

"But what if . . .?"

"Tomorrow we make ready for Spanish. Tonight we cook hen."

Asha-po was true to his word. Returning from a quick dawn trip through our tunnel to the creek, we wrapped our fresh catch of marsh hen and duck in damp palm fronds and laid them to roast beneath the embers of our fire. Our next meal attended to, we set about collecting the debris from the great storm. The hauling took most of the day. Other days followed in much the same pattern: first the early-morning journey to our traps, then immersion in the work of the colony. While neither Father nor the Colony of Carolina itself had set me to any task save the use of my eyes, I possessed a brain which schooled me otherwise. If the small gun were to be of any service against a true threat, it needed to be strategically placed and protected. Thus I devised my grand plan.

Carefully Asha-po and I notched and layered trunks of fallen palms lengthwise upon each other till we'd built our own little fortress—the first part of my grand plan. Near the end of our first week upon O'Sullivan's Island, we stood back to assess what we'd created.

We'd had enough trunks for only two walls, not

more than two yards high. They jutted at an angle toward the south—buttressed with sand rising above their base. To give the barrier more depth, we'd dug out the triangular interior till we penetrated the layer of hard, damp sand beneath. This we'd packed into a solid floor. It was the most modest of fortifications, yet we were quite pleased with the results of our labor.

Asha-po rapped the spongy wood. "Good wood. Catch arrows. Catch shot from guns of Spanish."

I squinted into the horizon. "Yes, the Spanish. We'd better get the cannon moved behind this barricade quickly. We can shoot it through our gun port in the corner."

The rough, window-like gap I'd built into the design pleased me. It had taken some thought and care. Sweating over the colony's palisade on the mainland hadn't hurt at all. I pictured the three-pounder's barrel protruding through the opening, red hot from spitting balls at the enemy, then shook the vision from my mind. The Spanish might never come. In the meantime our little fortress could have other uses.

"After settling the gun, at the first sign of bad weather we can batten down O'Sullivan's old canvas atop the walls. If another storm comes, it won't be as tight a roof as thatch, but it will give us some protection." I smiled. "And that's the rest of my grand plan."

"Is good plan," Asha-po approved.

◇          ◇          ◇

By sunset of that sixth day of sentry duty, we were organized to my satisfaction at last. With grunts and sweat we'd dug the imbedded wheels of the gun carriage from the sand and conveyed the three-hundred-and-fifty-odd pounds of bronze to its new home. It now stood at attention, muzzle aimed to shoot through its port toward the south. Surrounding the gun were our supplies of balls and gunpowder at the ready. I gave the neat pyramid of three-pound iron balls a proprietorial pat. Whether or not the Spanish came, Father could not berate me for laziness. I had done my duty.

We ate the remainder of the morning's catch until we could eat no more. I leaned back against a fortress wall to digest.

"You are right, Asha-po." I stroked my distended stomach. "This is no desert island. I haven't been as full since leaving England."

"Meat good," he said, "but must keep strong. Fort ready. Hard work over. Tomorrow find green things to eat."

"*Vegetables?*" I almost screeched. "Are vegetables really necessary?"

"No green things, no *vegetables*, teeth come loose. Fall out. No teeth, no eat. No eat, *die.*"

"Scurvy." I sighed. "I thought that only happened on the ocean. And I thought I had escaped *green things* by coming to this island. Not that my sister's watercress-and-wild onion salads were that dreadful . . ." I turned my head from the night sky to watch my friend. He was fussing over a small twig with his knife. "What are you doing?"

"Make for teeth." He held up the brush he'd made by fraying the ends, then set to scrubbing his teeth with it. "Asha-po clean teeth. No teeth, no eat."

"No eat, die." I chuckled. But I leaned forward. "Show me how to make a toothbrush, Asha-po. Your way seems much better than mine."

Come the morrow the wind shifted again. Now it came from the north. I peered carefully to the south anyway, but felt much less guilty about leaving my post on the beach to head inland for greens. We filled our bags with watercress and wild onions, then added wild carrots, too. Asha-po even introduced me to a curious plant with leaves akin to cabbage, but having an astonishing reek.

"*Peee-uw!*" I nearly gagged.

Asha-po smiled. "Is like skunk."

"That smelly, little animal with the white stripe down its back? The one we made the mistake of trapping last month?"

He nodded agreement, then poked around in the roots of the patch, collecting a handful of nut-like balls. "See." He made me inspect them. "Grind very small—"

"Grind into a powder?"

"Yes. Put little—not much—*powder* in hot, very hot water. Drink. Sickness here—" he pounded his chest and made a show of wheezing, "—goes away. Sickness of hot sweats goes away."

"So it is good for colds and fevers. I had best collect some for my mother."

We broke through the myrtle tunnel in midafternoon, joking about the very, very healthy stew we would be cooking that evening from our greens and a fat raccoon we had trapped. The sun beat on us again. The waves lapped comfortably along the shore. . . . And bearing down through shrieking gulls were two big ships.

## Thirteen

**"The Spanish!" I yelped.**

It had to be. The distinctive style of the hulls, with their high sides and towering sterncastles. The colors the ships were flying. The guns pointing ominously through open ports—more guns than any English merchantman carried. And glinting in the sun, vast, crescent-shaped blades affixed to the yardarms. Asha-po froze, staring at the ships as if he were slipping into another of his boat trances. I pounded him out of it. "Our gun! We've got to give the alarm!"

Asha-po snapped to life, and we raced across the sands to our little fortress. Would our mad dash be noticed? There was no time for worry on that account. Alas, there was sufficient time to worry over my neglect of sentry duty. My family would be at risk if I failed to give the alarm. The entire colony would be at risk. All because of *vegetables*.

"*Witling . . . Dunce . . .*" I huffed the words in rhythm to my headlong strides. Over and over. If my folly placed Mother and Julia in danger . . .

At last! Reaching our fortress walls, I tossed aside the pernicious greens. Tried to calm myself enough to perform the drill according to Colonel Godfrey's instructions.

*Powder first.*

I wrestled the top from the gunpowder barrel and poured a charge into the muzzle, shouting:

"Fire, Asha-po! Bring me fire from our embers!"

*Ram and ball.*

I wadded the powder and rammed it down the barrel before hoisting a ball and shoving it into the mouth of the cannon.

*Ram and pack.*

Using the rammer again, I packed all into the bottom of the bore.

*Vent and fuse.*

I dashed to the rear of the gun. Filled the vent with priming powder. Added a fuse.

Asha-po brought me fire. I took the flaming branch from him. "Stand back. The gun may be dangerous!"

*Fire!*

I lit the fuse. I watched the flame slowly eat its

way down the length of string. It disappeared into the vent. Holding my breath, I waited.

***BOOOOOOOM!***

Sound—and too many pounds of recoiling cannon—assaulted me at once. Coughing through the smoke, I picked myself up from the sand. Asha-po stood there beaming.

"Big noise. Very fine!"

Still hacking from the fumes, I poked my head over the top of our little fortress. All I had accomplished was a large splash farther out to sea.

"*Zoons*. I forgot to aim."

It was not something the Spanish would forget, though. Now alerted, the galleons were nosing closer to land. Already I could see swarms of men gathering above deck near those gun ports. I would have to do better.

"More fire, Asha-po! And hold on to it this time!"

Methodically I set about my second attempt. I worked my way through the drill, rammed home the powder and ball, primed the vent. But this time I added something to Godfrey's instructions: I paused to carefully point the cannon barrel directly at the hull of the nearest galleon. Satisfied, I retreated to the rear and held out my hand for the flame. Asha-po shoved it aside.

"I make shoot this time."

He did.

Together we rocked back from the impact. Together we raised our heads through the smoke till we were staring above our barricade. Together we watched the ball heave through the rigging of the ship. Together we watched the mainsail topple.

"*Zoons*," we breathed as one.

Then we ducked fast as the Spanish answered our fire.

By the sun, our little battle lasted for much of an hour. It lasted forever by any other method of time-keeping. The gun seemed to shoot high, so I continually readjusted its barrel in seeking the best range. Yet as the pyramid of balls grew smaller and smaller, we made but two more direct strikes against the enemy. With the other balls I fear we succeeded only in disturbing the creatures of the sea.

The aim of the Spanish gunners was better. Many balls flew barely past our heads, landing within yards of our unprotected rear. Fortune was with us. There was no damage beyond great eruptions of sand. Half a dozen ten-pounders thumped firmly into the wood of our defenses, but the barrier held strong. At last, O'Sullivan's Island's supply of powder and balls was finished. I turned to Asha-po. His bare chest was coated gray with sand, his bronzed face was streaked with smoke, and his eyes shown with war lust.

"Our ammunition is all gone," I said.

"No more?" the lust faded slightly.

I hoisted myself above the barricade a final time. "Look!"

Asha-po joined me. "Spanish go away."

The two ships had turned south, both limping from our damage. We watched as they ignored the entrance to the Colony of Carolina's bay. Watched as they chose to continue south to disappear into the mists of a lowering cloud bank.

"*Struth!*" I breathed. "We've single-handedly thwarted the Spanish! Saved the colony. Saved the Sewee."

Then we whooped.

"Chris-to-pher and Asha-po win battle!" Asha-po roared.

"The Battle of O'Sullivan's Island!" I bellowed.

"Kenato make story of battle." Asha-po's eyes were alive again, this time with pride. "Great story of great warriors—Sewee and English together."

I laughed. "And it will be told by the winter fire to our grandchildren when we are old and gray."

"Yes," Asha-po solemnly agreed. "Now we cook feast. War is hungry work."

It was fortunate that our raccoon was such a large one, fortunate the despised greens so abundant. The cloud bank into which the Spanish galleons had vanished moved north, bringing with it days of foul weather. Because of the rain, Asha-po and I spread canvas over our fortress. Within its shelter we succumbed to indolence following the battle which had topped our days of hard labor.

Knowing that my family was safe, I felt free to sleep till I could sleep no more. Knowing that our vigil was over, I felt free to relax until the colony chose to send the sloop for me. Also knowing their collective discomfort with the sea, I suspected the trip would not be made until the weather cleared. Praying the weather continued foul, I set about enjoying my windfall days with Asha-po. On the second morning I reached for my knife and began cutting a pattern into the hard sand of the floor.

"What is this you do, Chris-to-pher?" Asha-po lazily rotated his body in my direction.

I continued making grooves till I had a square filled with smaller checkered squares. "My father will send the sloop for me soon. While we wait for my rescue—"

"Rescue?" he asked. "Chris-to-pher need go back, Asha-po take in canoe."

"Ah, but I don't *need* to go back, do I? Asha-po doesn't *need* to return, either." I glanced up. "Do you?"

He caught on. Snickered.

"As I was saying, while we wait for my *rescue*, we are going to play draughts. It's a very fine English game. But we'll need playing pieces for it." I sheathed my knife and stretched. "For that we'll have to get wet."

"Wet?" Asha-po frowned with distaste.

"Only a very quick run through the rain. You must find twelve very small, flat stones—"

"*Twelve?*" he questioned.

I held out my hands. "Ten fingers plus two fingers. Twelve."

"Ah."

"And I must find twelve very small shells."

"With this we play English game?"

"Yes."

Asha-po nodded. "Very fine. Sewee love games. After English game I teach Sewee game."

"Perfect."

It was, almost. Asha-po took to draughts like a duck to water. Soon he was moving across the checkered spaces with glee. It took no time at all for him to grasp the concept of capturing the enemy. This he did with tremendous enthusiasm, much to my dismay.

"I win again, Chris-to-pher," Asha-po crowed. "See. I take prisoner your English shells."

"For the third time in a row," I grumbled. "I should have known you had a mind for military strategy. I'd hate to see what you could do with chess."

"Chess?" he inquired. "What is this *chess?*"

"Never mind. You promised to teach me a Sewee game next."

"Later. Chess first."

I shrugged acceptance. "We will need to make more pieces. These draughts pieces will do nicely for pawns, but we will need two kings, and two queens, and castles, and knights—"

"*King* I know. Not know *queen* . . . cas-el. . . ." He frowned. "*Night*? When sun father sleeps? How make night? Tell me, Chris-to-pher. It rains still. Waves still crash on water. There is much time."

His words were true. I settled back against a wheel of the cannon carriage and began explaining the mysteries of chess.

"You already understand that a *king* is an English chief. A *queen* . . ." I concentrated. "A *queen* is wife to the king, but very powerful. She is more like the earth mother. And a *knight* is a person, not the black sky with its stars and moon. A knight is a *warrior*."

"Ah. Is good to have warrior." He nodded with satisfaction. "We make shapes of these to play your chess."

"Yes. It is much more difficult than draughts. It is a true game of war."

Asha-po rose. "We go to tunnel. Find wood to make. My queen is earth mother, my king is sun father. Sun father holds more power than any chief!"

That made me smile. I was being challenged. Maybe the entire English system was being challenged. I glanced outside our tiny fortress shelter to verify what I already knew from the pounding on the canvas above us. "It is raining very hard now, Asha-po."

"Rain wakes us. Maybe food in traps."

"What, you grow tired of raccoon?"

"First day raccoon good. Second day raccoon not so good." He gestured toward our moldering remains. "Third day raccoon smell *peee-uw*."

I laughed. "I hope the stars are in the right conjunction with the moon, because I guess I'm getting a bath whether I want one or not."

Luckily Asha-po did not ask me to explain all of that. It would have taken the remainder of the afternoon.

For the next few days, while waiting for the sky to clear and the sea to calm, Asha-po and I sat carving little chess figures. As we worked I explained the significance of each and the strategies each was allowed to use in the game. I strongly suspected that my tiny statue of Charles II would give little competition to Asha-po's brilliant sun father with its fierce, round face surrounded by rays radiating like spikes. My queen, then, became the Glorious Elizabeth. Surely she could hold her own against the Sewee's earth mother. It became a contest. My armored knights against Asha-po's loinclothed warriors, my turreted castles against Asha-po's thatched council houses. The hardest to explain were the bishops.

I glanced down at the fresh hunk of soft wood

in my hand. I'd begun outlining the high, pointed hat and the crook of the Archbishop of Canterbury. "A bishop is a man in charge of religion."

"What is *ree-li-zun?*"

"Religion is how a person prays to God."

"Ah. Sun father. Earth mother."

"Yes. In England prayer is—" What was it? "—very organized."

My friend stared at me blankly.

I wracked my brain for a better way to explain this, remembering Julia and my days of catechism. "In England religion has many *rules*—orders that say, 'Do this. Do *not* do that.' Orders that tell the English how they must live their lives."

"English not know this in head?" He touched his. "In heart?"

I shrugged. "Some know. But it is the old way. There are big houses—fancy houses called churches—that everybody goes to once a week to pray. On the day we call Sunday."

"You honor your god only on Sunday? Not rest of days?" Asha-po glared at this insult to the Almighty. "Why need big house to talk to English god? He lives in sky and trees. He lives in everything with beauty."

Indeed, these were hard questions to answer. "It is just the way it is in England. The way it happened in all the countries across the ocean. And the bishop is the chief of the churches, the chief of the prayers, the chief of the rules."

"So." Asha-po made his decision. "Kenato is my bishop. Kenato prays *every* day."

I carved another groove into my wood. It would seem my Archbishop of Canterbury was going to have a difficult rival as well.

So obsessed did Asha-po and I become with all things pertaining to chess, that I paid little attention to the sea. I was convinced the Spanish had washed their hands of the tiny fortress on the tiny island. Since our ammunition was gone, it was not worth considering the alternatives. Likewise I pushed from my mind the return of the colony's sloop. When the time was ripe, Asha-po and his canoe could ferry me home. The time was not yet ripe. Our marathon games of chess became life.

We knew nothing but the sixty-four squares we'd cut into the hard sand as we sprawled under the heat of the sun when it returned at last. No splashing waves. No crying gulls. No curious sandpipers. Only our feverishly spinning brains.

"*Halloo!*"

"*Halloo, ashore!*"

"You speak, Chris-to-pher?"

"No," I mumbled. As expected, Kenato had my archbishop in deep trouble yet again. In Europe it would be cause enough for another Thirty Years War.

"***Halloo there!***"

I finally raised my head from the board of sand. And there was the sloop, closing in on the shore.

"*Zoons*. I'd near forgot."

Asha-po grunted. "Tell English go home. Too busy leave island."

"Would that I could." I backed the Archbishop of Canterbury into safe but cowardly retreat and rose.

"Christopher!"

It was Father himself, and with him Colonel Godfrey. Both men eyed Asha-po but said naught as my friend and I hauled the sloop onto the beach.

"Father." I took his offered hand after he'd eased himself to land, then was shocked by his quick embrace.

"You look well, son. You have done well."

This was no small praise coming from my father. "Thank you, sir. So the alarm was heard?"

"Not only that, but—"

The colonel clambered over the side to join us. "Our sentries spied the galleons limping south, lad," he said. "Fine work. Very fine work! We tracked them to St. Helens Island where they put in to repair their damage."

Father took up the narration. "Then Colonel Godfrey led a party of fifty volunteers—"

"Took 'em by surprise, we did!" Godfrey boomed. "Even with that armor. Demmed hot. Too demmed hot for the climate." He shook his head.

"What of the Spanish, Father?" I asked.

"Sent them packing," Godfrey beamed. "Won't be seeing the likes of them again anytime soon. And no casualties to speak of for our colony." He stared at his bare forearms. "Save for the heat rash. I'm for retiring armor, pikes, the lot. New country, new ways." He harrumphed and pivoted toward the barricade. "And what have we here? What have we here?"

I turned back to my father as Godfrey marched off on a tour of inspection. "Asha-po and I have been busy."

Father actually smiled. "So I see. Would you care to make your report?"

"My pleasure, sir."

I made it in full then and there, finishing with, "Mother and Julia are well?"

"Prospering, only worried for *your* safety. They would have me raise sail immediately upon the first sound of the gun, but every man was needed through the conclusion of the affair. Then the sea must calm itself."

Father studied the barricade, next the Spanish balls Asha-po and I had collected into small mountains. "Ten-pounders. Even a few twenty-four-pounders by their looks. The Spanish hit you hard."

I shrugged. "It was nothing. Asha-po and I were prepared."

"So it would seem." My father frowned for the

first time. "Perhaps my concern would have lessened had I known you had company in your labors." He glanced around. "But where has your Sewee gotten to? I believe he deserves some thanks."

"Asha-po?" I called.

No response.

"Asha-po!"

I did a quick search. His chess pieces were gone. His kit was gone. I turned to the sea. There was his canoe, bearing north. I worked out his route in my mind. He would skim around the island, then through the creek. He would want to remove our traps. What we could not eat would not be wasted. . . . With all that, he'd be in his village before I in mine. I wished mightily that I could be with him in that canoe. Yet I returned to my father.

"Asha-po has a shy nature. I will be pleased to convey your thanks to him."

"Do so."

Colonel Godfrey bustled up. "Amazing. Imagine that rascal O'Sullivan complaining of this isle. Slacker. Couldn't accomplish half what a mere lad *completed.*"

He rubbed his hands with enthusiasm.

"Best get this gun transported back to the colony. High time we began looking toward the land." Godfrey spun away from the barricade to focus on Asha-po's receding canoe. "Don't trust these demmed savages."

Fourteen

*Once the excitement of the Spanish scare ebbed,*
summer gradually blended into autumn. The crops
were gathered, and the corn was good. Seeing its
glory, I wished we had planted many more acres of
it. Our English seeds had not prospered.

Asha-po and I saw precious little of each other
during this harvest time for both villages. Our fortnight on O'Sullivan's Island was becoming more like
a dream with every passing day. While storing grains
and roots for the winter, I chafed for the moment I
would be freed to return to hunting. Father was looking to the wilderness as well, but with other thoughts.

"It is high time we moved forward to the surveying of lands for our plantation, Christopher," he
announced one evening over the meal. "With
Governor Sayle still ailing—"

"The poor soul has not set foot from his hut since it was nearly built around him," Mother interjected.

"And not likely to, either," Julia opined. "First it was ship weariness, then the ague, and this morning his servant girl Jane said a palsy has taken over all his limbs—"

"While Governor Sayle is ailing still," Father broke in, "for which we pray to Providence for his release—"

"Jane says the only release he'll be seeing is the grave." Julia reached for the water pitcher.

"Are you quite finished?" Father inquired. "May I proceed?"

Oblivious, Julia prattled on. "The old man's been lying abed muttering about where he wants his bones to rest. First he cries out, 'England!' Next, 'Bermuda!'—where he was governor first, and which was a much more civilized place than here—"

"Enough of Sayle and his infirmities!" Father burst out. "While I am still in charge of the colony, I have been given first choice of lands. We'll set off tomorrow, Christopher and I. I have hopes that the area along the Ashley River has soil less sandy than here."

I sighed. It was more than evident there would be no hunting for me until Father's latest itch was scratched. I tried to put some heart into the enterprise. "You mean to plant more corn in the spring?"

"*Corn*," he scoffed. "I am to grow corn when the

Proprietors have instructed me to cultivate cotton and indigo and cane roots?"

"You can *eat* corn, Father," Julia pointed out. "You cannot eat cotton and indigo."

It seemed a reasonable comment if one took into consideration the fact that we were currently supping on corn cakes. Mother added her reflections from her days in the common fields.

"Corn is all that appears to grow comfortably in this place, Joseph. That and the few wild gourds that sprang up among it this season—"

"I have no taste for these Indian gourds," Father complained. "They haven't the subtleties of an English marrow. And why do you suppose I seek less sandy soil? Next year's harvest will be better."

"We have few English seeds remaining to sow next year," Mother said. "And none of your indigo or cane."

"A supply ship will come." Father bit into his corn cake with finality. "We will leave just after dawn tomorrow, Christopher. I have arranged to borrow the colony's surveying equipment—along with our surveyor general."

"Mr. Culpepper?" I asked.

"The same. The man cannot be damned forever for his choice of servants. And all traces of Fitzpatrick do seem to have disappeared with the Spanish. Should our land search be fruitful,

Culpepper will be of use." He glanced up. "See that you are at hand and prepared to make camp."

With all the subjects Asha-po and I had discussed during our sojourn on O'Sullivan's Island, we had never gotten back to the issue of property rights. Asha-po had been correct about one thing in our earlier talk, though. There was much land. If one were only to use it as intelligently as the Sewee . . . My mind dwelt on this thought as I followed my father's lead the next morning.

By rights *I* should be in the lead, knowing the territory as I did. Instead I covered the rear, burdened with the weightiest of Mr. Culpepper's surveying tools. It suddenly struck me how long it had been since I had laid eyes on a horse. The commerce of London depended upon the horse. All of England relied upon it. Such a beast of burden would be useful at this moment. But until the hoped-for supply ship arrived, such beastly duties would fall upon the shoulders of the likes of me.

Even though we had begun early, it was noon before we'd fought our way through marsh and underbrush to where Lord Ashley's river emptied into the bay. I set down my load, flushed with the heat that remained in Carolina though it be early October now—and cool—in the England of horses. Father pulled the cork from his water bottle and drank deeply. "We will have a bite to eat, then move inland."

I'd been studying the land formation. "Upland." I pointed to a rise. "Away from the marsh and along the banks of the flowing river. The air will be more felicitous."

"Have it your way, Christopher. As long as the soil we test be less sandy." He turned to Culpepper. "My son has been formulating curious theories."

Culpepper was patting at his beet-red face with a handkerchief. He was a gaunt, petulant man, with sparse, ginger-colored hair that clashed with his current complexion. "As long as the choice be made. The rest of the colony waits upon it."

"Indeed." My father eyed the man with the distaste he had disavowed only the evening before. "Then perhaps we should not be taking our leisure here at all, but continue our march."

That set Culpepper aback, but I merely groaned and hoisted my load once more.

Father ended up choosing many acres encompassing and radiating from a small peninsula overlooking the Ashley River's channel. I could make no protest, for it was the highest elevation to be had. Father was satisfied because the soil was, indeed, less sandy than that surrounding the present colony. At sunset Culpepper pounded in the first boundary stake on a bluff jutting above the water, while I made a fire and supper. In the morning the surveying would commence. With it, I, too, would become a landowner at the expense of the Sewee.

Culpepper was still rolled in his blanket next to the embers of our fire when I woke with the dawn. I found my father standing with his back to the river, smoking a rare pipe of tobacco.

"There." He pointed the clay stem with satisfaction toward the mist-enshrouded forest. "There lies your hundred acres, son. And mine, and your mother's, and your sister's. 'Tis a fair sight. A fair beginning after all our travails."

I nodded acceptance. Father may have chosen my acres as well as his, but it was I who had directed his search to the edge of Sewee territory. "And what of Lord Ashley's land?" I asked.

"Beyond. His ten thousand acres lie beyond."

"Not that he's ever likely to see them."

"No. Yet I'll tend the parcel well for him. As shall you as my heir. But the establishment of the West plantation—our four hundred acres—will come first. It is only just. The journey and the sweat should count for something."

Before I could make answer, a figure strode noisily toward us.

"What have you done with my compass, boy?

And my chain?"

It was Culpepper, scratching at his bristly chin. The private moment with my father evaporated.

"Still where they were left yesterday, sir. On the far side of the fire."

"Fetch them and let's be done with the task."

I caught my father's eye. Was I to be treated no better than a servant or beast of burden by this man? Father's expression had hardened, but he gave me an imperceptible nod that spoke worlds. He understood my plight, yet I was to play the part still. I was to submit to this one, too. Had my conduct on O'Sullivan's Island counted for naught? How was it that Asha-po was already a man among his people, yet I must wait another five years for the respect which would come with my own majority?

Father read the emotions in my hesitance.

"Christopher—"

"Yes, sir." It wasn't a horse I'd become, but a donkey.

If the surveyor's chain had been heavy as I had carried it the day before, it became heavier still in use. It was a simple measuring device made of one hundred iron links measuring sixty-six feet in length. I stood before the first boundary post, holding the chain by its handles. "What do you wish me to do, Mr. Culpepper?"

He glanced up from the open compass on his palm. "Do? Have you not read your Euclid?" he rasped. "Have you not had the geometry?"

I nodded. Indeed, I had. Both. But John Hawkes had never revealed to me the uses for vulgar arithmetic, nor the purpose of squares and triangles over the degrees of whose angles I'd labored.

"Eighty chains make one mile," Culpepper barked. "Ten square chains make one acre. I will sight true north from this boundary point. You will convey the chain in direct lines following the compass needle until we have surveyed the acreage. First that of the West family. Next that of Lord Ashley."

I turned toward the forest. "A straight line through the trees?"

"Should a tree block our line of site, you will either chop it down or I will site on the trunk, walk around, and approximate the continuing line."

Never before had the forest been unwelcoming to me. Yet as I began that day with chain and ax under Culpepper's tutelage, I could have wished it as bare as most of O'Sullivan's Island.

Father returned to the affairs of the colony, leaving me as drudge to Culpepper. Many's the moment in the course of the next few days when I could have wrung the man's skinny neck as easily as Asha-po had dispatched our first marsh hen. Yet by the time of our own return to the colony, I had learned much of the art of surveying. And learned, too, that it was the surveyor who brought the true death knell to the wilderness. It was a skill I relinquished as willingly as the heavy weight of the iron chain.

"Here." I dropped all one hundred links of it outside Culpepper's door.

He paused beneath the lintel to give his brow a final swab. In five days' time his handkerchief had gone from a starched white to a very unhealthy gray.

"Inform Mr. West that I shall have his headrights platted in due course. Also remind him that the survey fee is a half penny per acre. Sterling." Culpepper squinted through the afternoon brightness. "With the addition of eleven shillings and eight pence upon setting the papers in his hands. Have you understood that, boy?"

"I certainly have, sir."

The message could wait. My homecoming could wait. I set off for a swim in the sea to wash away the entire experience.

## Fifteen

*"Good,"* *Asha-po grunted when I turned up at his* village the next morning with my bow and quill of arrows.

"It is time to hunt, isn't it?"

"Yes."

But he continued running a soft skin cloth over something hidden on his lap. His mother emerged from the hut behind to shove a packet of food in my hand. "Chris-to-pher take Asha-po far away from *that.*"

She pointed at the object which Asha-po now revealed. It was a handsome chessboard with lovingly inlaid squares of colored wood. She shook her head.

"Mother think chess make me foolish," Asha-po announced.

I laughed. "It is a far better way to spend your

time than what I've been doing the past few days."

"What?" he asked.

"Get your bow," I ordered. "I'll explain as we search for game."

"We play chess?" he begged. "After we bring home deer?"

"Yes. After we bring home deer."

The game of chess commenced sooner than expected, but it was not destined to be played upon Asha-po's fine, inlaid board.

It was a perfect autumn day, crisp and finally cool. We slipped into the arms of the forest to tread lightly upon fallen leaves of red and yellow intermingled with faded needles of pine. We paused as a deer danced past. I reached for an arrow from the quill slung over my shoulder.

Asha-po shook his head. "No."

Thinking he had something grander in mind, I released my grip and followed. Deeper yet we penetrated the wilderness. Sun shone through the overhead canopy of trees like rays slanting through the stained-glass windows of a cathedral, sprinkling us with crimson and gold. The silence was mighty. Powerful. I paused again with Asha-po in stillness beside me to breathe a prayer of praise to God, and the earth mother, and the sun father—

A twig crackled underfoot.

Asha-po yanked me behind the cover of the nearest tree.

"A buck?" I whispered. A prodigious buck is what I wished for. A buck with more points on his head than a stag my father and I had spied on Lord Ashley's estate. I would drag it home in triumph. Its antlers would decorate the wall behind my cot. . . .

Asha-po soundlessly nocked an arrow in answer. He tensed his bowstring. Not knowing what to expect, I followed suit. What happened next came with a suddenness beyond understanding. A figure moving with great stealth emerged from the foliage. Asha-po's string twanged. The figure fell, barely breaking the silence. Then Asha-po was no longer beside me, but hovering above his kill.

"What?" I crept over to him and looked. It was an Indian. A *man*!

Already Asha-po had retrieved his arrow, leaving bloody bubbles gushing from his victim's heart.

"You killed him!"

Asha-po clapped his hand on my mouth. "Hide body," he ordered.

I locked my jaw against the sudden heaving of my stomach and grabbed for the man's legs. Like an automaton I helped remove the dead Indian from the little clearing. Dropped my half of the burden. Dropped the contents of my stomach. Wiped my mouth and looked to Asha-po for an explanation.

"See." He pointed at his victim's face. "Paint for war," he whispered. "Is Westo. One who comes before others."

"A scout," I murmured.

Asha-po shrugged. "Scout. *Pawn.* More pawns come. Then knights, bishops, king. Come for Sewee harvest. Come for English harvest. Come for war."

He pulled out his knife and bent over the Westo. When he straightened up again, he had an ear in his hand. My empty stomach roiled into cramps as I stared in horror and fascination at the bloody flesh. Then I raised my eyes to those of my friend's. The war lust was back. This time it was deeper than I could fathom.

Asha-po punched me. "Wake up, Chris-to-pher. We take news to my village. To your village. Maybe we kill more pawns on the way."

"But you're supposed to *capture* pawns!"

"Not when pawn is Westo." Asha-po kicked the fallen warrior. "Westo bad fierce. Westo capture Sewee, take more than ear. Take skin, take scalp—" he pointed to his groin, "—take manhood. Take *all* while Sewee alive. *Then* Westo kill."

The forest cathedral turned chill around me. I stumbled through naught but darkness to its edge and the waiting colony.

Colonel Godfrey had his militia in formation on the beach parade ground within the hour of my return.

"Right!" he barked. "Joseph West is in command of the palisade, with Samuel Bull and George Culpepper in second and third command." Godfrey paced before the line, halting at its far side where the remainder of the colony members were gathered. He scowled at the weeping females.

"First order of the day is to collect all women and children within the safety of the fortress walls. The food and water in readiness will serve for a week-long siege should worse come to worst."

He about-faced to inspect his troops. A few wore armor helmets, but their bodies were protected otherwise with naught but flintlocks and the quilted vests he'd had the women sewing since the Spanish engagement. He'd been drilling the men since then, too. Several hours a day he'd forced them under the hot sun. The results brought no noticeable improvements in their military demeanor aside from the growth of their capacity to swear. As ordered, I stood at attention among them, having been restored to my senses since breaking through the forest with my news. I still did not merit a flintlock, but I'd slung my bow and quiver over the vest that had been foisted upon me, along with my forsaken boots.

"The rest of you," Godfrey shouted, "prepare to march!"

I shook my head in sorrow.

"Don't march in formation!" I'd begged Godfrey once my tale of the coming Westo invasion was told.

"Send the men out in small groups of two or three. This is how the Indian fights. He hides, then chooses his victim." As Asha-po had.

"Nonsense, Master West. We'll show the demmed Westo our strength. The strength of the English!"

Thus it was that I re-entered the forest with the strength of the English. Worse, I re-entered it with Colonel Godfrey's ringing cry: "Beat up the drum and bid the heathens to battle!"

Colonel Godfrey may have had a wish for death, but I did not. Our drum beats would summon every Westo within miles—not for battle, but for ambush. In vain I considered ways to silence the drum's sharp staccato. The problem was solved by the Westo themselves—at least one Westo arrow. Shortly into our march it came flying through the column to strike the drummer in his shoulder. Bedlam broke out, in the midst of which my boot unaccountably smashed through the tight skin of the Colony of Carolina's sole military drum.

"Re-form! Re-form!" bawled Godfrey. "We'll teach the enemy to fight openly!"

Too late. His troops were ducking for cover. In less than an hour the effects of the drum and the wilderness had accomplished what my earlier pleas to Colonel Godfrey had not. Our force had been separated as if planned by my own strategy.

I found myself in an isolated pocket of jungle straddled between William and Burnaby Bull, the kinsmen and servants of Samuel Bull, when I heard the first belated English shot in answer to the Westo arrow. Burnaby Bull's face crumpled in terror. William Bull's legs did what his face did not—they collapsed, leaving him in a pile upon the forest floor. I tore off the vest that obstructed me. Tossing the hateful object aside, I next yanked off my boots. I flexed my bare feet. Now I could move again.

"Quickly," I goaded the two. "The shot was not far in advance. We'd best place ourselves to fight."

"Where?" wailed William Bull.

I studied our position. It was no better nor worse than it could be. We were in a heavily forested area. Any of the trees could be hiding Westo. They could be behind us as well as before us. Thanks to Godfrey's drum summons, they could be surrounding us.

Another shot rang out.

"*Splood*," moaned Burnaby Bull. "'Make your fortune!' me mum says, as she shoves me aboard ship. Being swineherd ain't bad enough, now the heathens'll do me in. Curses on this damned Paradise!"

"Shut your mouth, you great hulk," I commanded. "Follow me and learn to fight like a real man. Like an Indian." I pointed to the ancient live oak sprawled behind us. "Climb it."

"A *tree*?" William Bull asked.

I could tarry no longer. Aiming a kick at his hefty buttocks, I sprang up the trunk as if born to it. I was already well settled, bestriding an outer branch with a view and room for my bow, when the third shot rang out. It was followed by a flurry of shots and a high-pitched scream. William and Burnaby Bull scrambled after me like squirrels.

My arrow in readiness, I waited, wishing with all of my being that Asha-po was beside me instead of these two fools. Yet perhaps his spirit was with me. When the moment arrived, I was able to act with his coolness of purpose.

Within five minutes, Florence O'Sullivan burst through the branches in full retreat as if the devil himself were at his heels. A Westo followed in close pursuit, hatchet raised for the final blow. I let fly my arrow. O'Sullivan crashed on without a backward look as the Indian dropped.

*Zoons.* I'd gotten my buck.

The realization hit hard. So hard, the air was taken out of me, and I nearly dropped my weapon. It was the Bulls who saved me then.

"Did you see that? Robin Hood of Sherwood Forest could have done no better."

"Right between the shoulder blades!"

"Silence!" I hissed. My breath returned, but my entire body throbbed with the beating of my heart. I reached for another arrow.

⟡　　　⟡　　　⟡

Early darkness started closing in as we stiffly clambered down the tree. Three bodies awaited us.

"Lookit this one, Burnaby!" William exulted. "This be the savage you shot with the flintlock." He stepped aside. "You get the honors, coz."

I was at Burnaby before his knife was fully pulled from its sheath. "What are you doing?" I growled.

"I'm just after a scrap of him, a little memento—"

"No! Are you not better than those you call heathens?"

"Sblood, Christopher West. Tend to your own savages."

Fatigued as I was, I never once considered that Burnaby was near twice my size. I merely laid into him with a punch to the chin that knocked him onto the forest floor. Then I stood back, rubbing my knuckles.

"We will be *civilized*."

Burnaby shook his head. Half-dazed, he pushed himself up. "Whatever you say, West." He gave his victim's body a final look of longing. "Would taking his hatchet be all right?"

I sighed. "By all means help yourself to the hatchet." I turned to leave.

"Hey! Where are you off to?" William complained.

"Home."

"You cannot be leaving without us! We'll never find our way out of this maze!"

It was a truth which had occurred to me. I paused, torn between duty and the real destination I had planned—Asha-po's village. I needed to know if he was still in the game. And if he was still in the game, I needed to know if we'd gotten past the opening moves to its middle phase. Of only one thing I was certain: we hadn't yet reached game's end with the Westo.

"Come, then. Now. And keep your tongues and feet silent. The enemy can shape itself into the very trees."

Sixteen

*I slept that night within the walls of the palisade.*
It was a fitful sleep, surrounded as I was by the
groans of the English casualties. By God's grace we
had not lost a single man; by God's mercy—and
chance. I could not ascribe it to competence. Yet
there would be fewer able to take on the Westo in
the morning. It wasn't the wounded who troubled
my sleep, though. It was the *unthinkable* waiting just
beyond the fortress walls.

This discovery had I made on returning from my
day at war: Dr. Henry Woodward and his stalwart
followers keeping watch over the Westo they held in
captivity. The warriors were trussed like chickens,
yet every inch of their anatomies soundlessly spewed
forth fury and hatred. Forgetting my lack of majority not for the first time, I'd approached the doctor.

"What are you doing?"

"As you see." He gestured toward the half-dozen Indians. His thin lips curled in a sly smile. "Our colony's labor shortage has been addressed. With the morrow I hope to strengthen the numbers."

"You'll hold the Westo as servants?"

Woodward was a handsome man of some thirty years, slim, and not great in stature, yet well appointed. His fine, almost aristocratic nostrils tightened in a sniff.

"Servants?" he sneered. "*Slaves.* They'll do until our commerce improves in a year or two and we can place an order for our first shipload of Africans." He turned his glance back toward the Westo.

"Slaves?" I breathed. "You cannot tame an Indian!"

"No matter. If they be sullen workers, there is still naught to be lost. I will march them north to Virginia and sell them there. Virginia planters are desperate for any hands whatever in their tobacco fields."

"But . . ."

Dr. Woodward waved me off. More fatigued than I'd ever been, I had forced myself to the palisade gate. *Pawns.* Once again Asha-po was in the right. It was far better to kill the enemy outright than to send his spirit into slavery. As for the Africans to come . . . Sick to my very soul with such thoughts, added to the burden of what I'd done that day, I had reeled into the palisade to the welcome of my family.

◇          ◇          ◇

"*Noooooooooooooo* . . ."

Nightmarish visions of gaping wounds, hovering spirits, endless columns of chained men . . . with such were my dreams filled.

"*Christopher!*" My sister Julia shook me. "Stop screaming, Christopher!"

I stirred. Tried to shake the ghastly images away. "Screaming?"

"You'll wake the entire palisade." She was whispering now. "And it's not nearly dawn."

Such rest was not worth pursuing. Casting off my blanket, I rose to stumble past bodies packed in sleep like cod in a salting barrel. I made my way to the foot of the steps rising to the fifth embrasure of the fortress. I climbed two stairs toward the forest gun port when a hand touched my arm.

"Wait, Christopher." It was Julia. "I can't sleep, either."

At the top, my sister and I leaned over the wooden parapet. The sharpness of the night air cleared the visions from my troubled brain. I rubbed the edges of a headache from my temples as we stared into the dark mass of trees before us.

"I know it wasn't the same as for you, Christopher," she began, "but it was bad here, too, yesterday. The women were hopelessly in fits—all save Mother."

I turned to my sister. "Mother?"

"She was like a fine lady . . . no, she was like a *queen*. She spent the day calming vapors, lecturing valor, comforting children, organizing meals. All with the most amazing bearing. *Regal* bearing, as if she'd waited an entire lifetime to turn from a mouse into a, a—"

"A lioness?" I asked. "And you, little sister?"

Julia sighed. "I believe I 'rose to the occasion.' That's what Mother said halfway through the endless afternoon. When it was the worst. We could hear the shooting, Christopher, but knew not what it meant. All those silly women were moaning about being raped and pillaged by savages—" Julia stopped. "*Pillage* I understand, but what does *rape* mean?"

"Never mind. What of Father?"

Julia sighed again, this time in frustration. But she didn't belabor the issue. "Father manned this very gun. Samuel Bull the other nearest the land."

"And Culpepper?"

She snorted quite an unladylike snort. "Mr. Culpepper manned a third gun. At least that was his given duty. When I brought him food and drink, I found him curled around the gun carriage in a worse state than any of the women."

"Does Father know of this?"

The dark silhouette of her head shook. "That was when our militia began staggering out from the trees. Culpepper brushed the dust from his breeches and strode down into the fortress as if he had saved the day himself."

"The cowardly knave—"

Julia nudged me. "Look!" She was whispering again. "Something odd about the forest . . ."

I followed her pointing finger. Something odd, indeed. It seemed to be growing outward, like Birnam wood come to Dunsinane. "The Westo!" I yelped. "And they knowing naught of Shakespeare's *Macbeth*! Give the alarm, Julia! I'll load the gun!"

So it happened that the fiery report of my cannon brought in the dawn on the second day of our war against the Westo.

There were many Westo. Far more Westo than English. Far more Westo than Sewee. Seemingly unending numbers of them advanced from the trees as the sun rose in the sky to join the brightness of exploding cannons and flintlocks. And they were brave. The deaths of comrades did not stop them. Instead it seemed to incite them to greater valor. Whooping great, blood-curdling whoops, the Westo leaped over their fallen and kept coming on. When they neared the very walls of the palisade and our guns could do no more harm, I turned to my bow. The foremost warriors were closing in on their brothers in captivity who still lay bound where

Woodward had abandoned them in his mad dash to enter the safety of the fortress.

I tensed my bowstring and took aim. Let fly the arrow. Watched it strike home. Took up another arrow without pause for thought or breath and took aim again. Let fly. Raised my eyes only long enough to note something new. A warrior to the rear of the advancing party was aiming a different kind of arrow. This one would carry with it fire.

Fire.

The enemy which had laid London low. Now I would meet it again. It was an enemy deadlier for a wooden palisade than hordes of Westo. My fingers froze to my bow, my very will in thrall to the bright flicker of chaos to come. Then Asha-po's chessboard forced its way into my mind. In chess a castle could move but forward or backward. Yet even of wood, it could make defense.

I nocked another arrow to the bowstring and aimed toward the fire bearer. Sighting down the arrow's length from my height above the battle-ground, I knew futility. The target was beyond my range. Such was not the case for the Westo's flaming missile. The warrior's bow was longer than mine. His strength was far greater. I hesitated, waiting for the moment he would set free the beginning of the end—

"*Zoons!*"

Before my eyes, the Westo fell. An arrow rose

perpendicularly from his back. I followed the sight-line farther to the rear, to the forest itself—

Another line of Indians emerged from the trees, a shower of arrows announcing its advance.

"The Sewee!" I cried. "The Sewee have come to our aid!"

"Quickly, quickly, Sewee warriors move forward."

Asha-po re-enacted the crucial battle upon his chessboard.

"Surround Westo at sea." He moved his king one space. "Father sun rises, shines his power in face of enemy. Westo now blind."

Asha-po swung his bishop diagonally across the open space. "Kenato raises song. Arrows fly. Westo snared."

He swept the board of its pieces and raised his eyes to smile, to utter the last words.

"End of game."

My friend had left out a few critical moments of the battle. He had left out the English crossbows and flintlocks taking careful aim from the palisade's parapets and arrow slits. He had left out the moment our gate swung open and the colony's men lunged forth in hand-to-hand combat with the enemy—an enemy trapped between the Sewee's main and flanking forces and the forest to the west, and the sea to the east. Neither had he mentioned the gathering of the

last of the Westo into snarling, spitting captives to
swell Dr. Woodward's reserve of slave labor.

"The Sewee did well," I replied.

I crooked my neck to gaze up the length of Asha-
po's war spear. It was rammed into the earth in a
place of honor before his family's hut. Carefully
laced to its length were six ears, drying in the sun.
My mind swirled back to our days of fishing by the
stream, when trout was matched by trout on our two
strings. The only mementos I could count from this
new competition were within me. They were
wounds of conscience that could equal and even better Asha-po's proud coups.

"Your chief," I spoke. "Sipio. Is he satisfied with
the colony's gifts?"

It had been late afternoon when all was finished.
The unforgettable scene played through my mind as
if I were living it again. North of the clearing outside
the palisade, dead Westo had been piled for burial.
Dead Sewee—numbering but a handful—lay waiting to the south to be returned to the forest for
proper rites. Dead colonists—two Barbadians and
the luckless Burnaby Bull—were lying in state
within the palisade. Inside the closer circle, Dr.
Woodward and his cohorts stood guard over the
Westo captives to one side, while the remaining
Sewee squatted in expectation of their just rewards
to the other. In the center stood my father.

"Christopher West." He summoned me.

Mother and Julia had only just seen to my wounds. I tried to ignore the blood seeping through bandages on both arms as I approached him. "Yes, sir?"

"Your friends. The Sewee. They seem to expect some form of compensation for their efforts."

"They did save our lives, Father."

"Too true." Father rubbed his cheek. "But what?"

"Iron axes. Hoes and rakes. Steel knives."

"You know we haven't enough of any of these!"

"A token, Father. Present their chief and medicine man with a token of each—with the promise of more when the supply ship arrives. One tool for every warrior who fought with us today."

"That will satisfy them?"

I studied the ranks of Sewee. Among them was Asha-po. He captured my glance and held it. I broke away from his grave stare.

"It is the best we can do. Their chief is named Sipio. He must be called forth. Also Kenato, their priest and medicine man." I touched my father's shoulder, no longer such a height above mine; caught his eyes. "They must be treated with utmost respect, Father. As if you were receiving them at Whitehall Palace before King Charles himself."

I turned to leave. This time it was my father's hand which caught *my* shoulder. "Order the implements collected, then return to my side, Christopher."

"Yes, sir."

When all was in readiness, Father squared his shoulders, threw back his great, dark mane of hair, and lifted his voice.

"I call forth Sipio, great *cacique* of the Sewee. I call forth Kenato, who holds the wisdom of the Sewee."

Father did deference well. It must have come from rising above years of submission. It must have come from finally casting aside his role as second son and growing into his own place and sense of power. As Sipio and Kenato strode proudly forward, Father bowed to each in turn. He made his speech of thanks. He made his presentations. I translated all.

"*Chris-to-pher.*"

"What?" I pulled my eyes from Asha-po's spear, and my thoughts from the events of but two days past.

"Sipio is satisfied with promise of gifts to come with big ships. Kenato is satisfied. My father is satisfied he will have steel knife. Like Asha-po." He grinned. "My mother is satisfied. I promise *her* my warrior choice will be iron hoe." His grin disappeared. "Lost warriors bad. Lost corn bad—"

"*What* lost corn?"

He gestured toward a blackened circle at the edge of the village. In my preoccupation I'd ignored the missing storehouse, even though pale wisps of smoke still rose from its ruins. So. Asha-po's story was more complex as well.

"How?" I asked.

Asha-po shrugged. "After battle, Sewee sad for dead warriors, much weary from fight. Kenato prepares the dead. Sewee sleep." He touched the discarded queen next to his chessboard. "But earth mother gives warning. Owl hoots. Lone Westo pawn escapes battle, seeks revenge. He cannot carry corn. He destroys with fire." Another shrug. "Half winter food gone. Soon Westo pawn gone, too."

"I am sorry for your corn."

His expression was stoic. "Better than whole village burned."

"Like the last harvest season."

A nod. "But Westo come no more this year. Tomorrow we hunt other beasts. Today we play real game of chess."

"Yes."

I had expected as much. I opened my leathern pouch to retrieve the pieces I'd brought. We began laying them out in ranks upon Asha-po's board.

# Seventeen

Dr. Henry Woodward worked his Westo slaves like teams of draft animals. In harness. Unlike draft animals, they fought against the leather that held them in bondage—silently, furiously, impotently. Against every protest I could make, it was determined that these captives were to labor on the recently surveyed West plantation.

After Dr. Woodward himself informed me of this plan, I accosted my father in his new office within the palisade. Perhaps recent events had given me a touch of wisdom, for I did not approach my father in the full heat of my fury. Instead, as John Hawkes had been at pains to teach me, I first attempted to build a logical argument. I began with studied outrage.

"How could you use them so unjustly, Father? These Westo are men like us!"

He set his quill on the planed boards that served as his desk. Slowly he sanded the wet ink on the page before him. "Not like us. They are savage, and they are the enemy. Were our roles reversed, I have little doubt that our outcome would be far worse." Carefully he tapped the sand from his ledger sheet.

Next I tried the Christian, humanitarian approach. "'They that are delivered from the noise of archers . . . there shall they rehearse the righteous acts of the Lord.'"

"*Judges.*" Father glanced up. "Your sudden interest in scriptures is gratifying, Christopher. I would not have expected it from you."

I would not have, either, but after leaving Woodward tending his captives, I had spent the entire morning in search of verses opposed to slavery in the family Bible. I could find none. Even after the travails of the Israelites in Egypt, within those holy pages *there was no opposition to the act of enslavement.* In desperation, I'd opted for compassion.

"Still," Father continued, "I am not swayed. As you are now a biblical scholar, you might also recall *Psalm Two.* 'Ask of me, and I shall give thee the heathen for thine inheritance, and the uttermost parts of the earth for thy possession.'"

*Thou shalt break them with a rod of iron; thou shalt dash them in pieces like a potter's vessel.* This next verse of the psalm I knew as well, but I recited it only to myself. Hadn't it upset me sufficiently during the course of my morning's research?

My final attack was based on family pride. I firmly squared myself before my father and his desk throne. "Would you then have the West plantation—the very name of *West*—be based for future generations upon the labor of *slaves*?"

Father wearily rubbed his brow. "Four hundred West acres, Christopher. Another ten thousand belonging to Lord Ashley. Two sets of hands—yours and mine. Tell me how many lifetimes we must live to clear this land."

He gave me no chance to make answer.

"The Westo are not our personal property, but that of the colony as a whole. They merely begin their labors upon our land. The means are not as I would have chosen, but I must learn to live with them. So must you."

He stared long and hard at me planted so defiantly before him.

"Affairs of the colony keep me here. You must be my factor on the plantation. You must oversee the clearing of the land for spring planting. You must oversee the building of the house."

"*What!*" This was a turn of events I had not foreseen. All my energies had been focused on my hopeless moral quest. Some of the righteous iron left my spine, and I clutched for the support of Father's desk. "But the hunting season has only begun—"

"Enough play, Christopher. Others may hunt. How oft have you complained of not being treated as an adult? I am giving you your opportunity."

"Haven't I already proven myself against the Spanish, proven myself against the Westo?"

"War is only another game, son. Like your chess. Real life—daily living—is different. Learn how it feels to take its burden upon your shoulders."

It was a heavy burden, indeed. With Henry Woodward and his captives, I set up camp on West land. The clearing began. With it began our disputes. Woodward would have every tree in sight felled. It was easier so, he believed.

"I am the factor," I proclaimed. "I will say which trees fall and which trees stand."

It was not much of an assertion of either my rights or my majority, but it was the best I could do. The grandest of trees around the house site I marked with my knife so they might be preserved. Their shade would hold some coolness on the hottest summer days. As for the future fields, I marked out slim rows of trees between them to be retained as natural fences.

"Stupidity!" Dr. Woodward exclaimed. "It will make the work harder, and every inch of possible field space should be made available."

I shrugged. "There is much land."

Work continued. The stumps had to be pulled from the house site, and the Westo did this like oxen yoked to a plow, staggering before a wheeled lever we devised. For the rest, they chopped and sawed from sunup to sundown. The Indians never uttered a word. They only strained, always under Woodward's eye and Woodward's flintlock—or that of his cohort, Ian Smith, who spelled the doctor. The fields began to look like nothing but barren desert, sprinkled with two-foot-high stumps of trees.

"Why?" I protested.

"Even my Indians are not enough to pull all these stumps, Christopher West," Woodward replied. "You will sew and reap between the stumps. In the fullness of time, the stumps will rot back into the earth. Your fields will be clear."

I watched the Westo maiming the forest—even worked beside them. At each day's end I compared the results of my labor to theirs. It paled into insignificance. Lying within my blanket at night, I suffered the aches of my strained muscles. Far worse, I suffered the aches of my conscience. Until exhaustion overtook me I fought the battle of my own beliefs with those of my father again and yet again. I was unwilling to concede him the right. Yet the evidence of my eyes—the labor of my two hands—proved the truth of his words. One man was not enough. Two men were not enough to prepare the land. It must be prepared, must it not? Was that not why our number had voyaged to this far country?

Soon a good thirty acres of the West plantation were prepared in this fashion—more than enough to tend in the coming planting season. I was grateful for the reprieve given the other three hundred and seventy acres. I yearned to disappear into them. But my compulsory term as factor was not yet completed. I'd also been charged with overseeing preparations for the West manor house. Accordingly, planks were split for its walls. And when these were enough, more planks were split.

"Why?" I asked Woodward.

He pointed to the bluff overlooking the river. "Until a road be made, the lumber will be cast into the Ashley to float downstream. It will be collected at its mouth. The wood will become cargo for the next ship."

October passed into November, then December. Asha-po came to visit once. He stood staring at the denuded fields and laboring Westo as he had stared at the big ships. His eyes left them only to stray toward Woodward and his flintlock, then back to me.

"*What?*" I growled.

Asha-po turned his back on the despoiled and the enslaved and returned to the forest.

◇    ◇    ◇

Two weeks before Christmas our new home was raised. For this, Father and Mother and Julia arrived. With them came half the colony: carpenters, roofers, every skilled workman we laid claim to. Westo hauled. Builders built. In but a few days the structure was complete. It was not quite the manor house Father had dreamed of upon paper, but it had eight rooms and a veranda encircling it. A kitchen and two-hole privy rose to its rear. When finished, Father studied it all with satisfaction.

"What say you, Elizabeth?"

My mother gazed at the house, at the desolation of stripped forest beyond, at the encroaching wilderness on every side but the river behind her. Tears slipped down her cheeks.

"Now, now, my dear." Father patted her. "I know you have been longing for your own home once more, but such gratitude is unnecessary. Christopher oversaw most of the work—"

"Father," Julia spoke. "Mother is not being grateful. Mother is frightened."

"Thank you, Julia." Mother finally spoke for herself, showing a little of the lioness which had been unleashed during the Westo War. She turned to Father. "The home can be made lovely, Joseph, and for this I thank you. But where is the palisade? Where are the guns? Where is our protection, half a day's journey as we are from the rest of the colony?"

She paused only long enough to add steel to her final words. "I cannot live here. My daughter cannot live here."

Father stood dumbfounded.

At last, I broke the painful silence. "Work can't begin in the fields for another month or more. By then the supply ship should arrive. It will have more colonists for company. It will have horses to make the journey to and from the sea shorter—"

"Yes, yes." Father found his voice again. "Perhaps with the spring all will appear different."

So it was that the West family temporarily abandoned its plantation to return to the security of the colony by the sea. Dr. Woodward drove his slaves to the next piece of wilderness to ravish—his own chosen plantation lands. And I planned the apologies for my reunion with Asha-po.

Eighteen

"*You spoke true about the land so many moons ago,* Chris-to-pher. About this thing you call *property*."

I had tracked Asha-po to the marshes where he was laying traps. Now he stood aloof from me on a hummock of dry land, arms folded, face chiseled granite.

"I did not believe. I did not believe English have such big stomachs. Stomachs that make Sewee forests desert. Stomachs that kill *all* Sewee deer."

He continued the list of atrocities committed against his way of life as if he had been practicing it as long as I had been practicing my apologies.

"I did not believe English have such hate for trees. I did not believe you have such hate for trees. For earth mother."

I held my silence. He was not yet finished. Had his arms not been folded so tightly, I could imagine him ticking off the next nefarious deed. It came anyway.

"Westo bad, yes. But even Westo not worse than snake. Even Westo have spirit. Break spirit, what is left?" His hands unfolded and he mimicked one of Woodward's slaves—bent, struggling against invisible bonds of rawhide. The light went out of his eyes, and with it the intelligence, as he contorted his body into the hollow skeleton of a man.

"Stop!" I begged.

Asha-po became Asha-po again. He crossed his arms once more. "Torture better. Ear gone, skin gone, a man is still a man."

I fought through his glare. "Have you come to the end of your grievances at last?"

He considered, then nodded. I took a deep breath. Now it was my turn. My turn to justify my own role in the English cruelty to man and nature.

"Asha-po—"

His face returned to stone. Seeing the hardness, all my excuses disappeared. They were worthless anyway. What good to try to explain yet again the English lust for land wealth? What good to justify my grudging supervision of the clearing of the family plantation, torn as I was between hating the destruction—yet growing to understand my father's truthful words? I had both fought and accepted my father's orders within myself. Without the Westo, the fields would have taken years to clear.

"Please try to understand, Asha-po—"

Suddenly my strength disappeared. Legs crumpling, I found myself kneeling upon the spongy moss of the hummock. The weight of life had become the weight of the world and all its injustices. I could not atone for the Englishness in me. I longed for Sewee simplicity. I was becoming neither. My fist grasped for a rock as if it would save me. I raised it, then bashed its sharp edges at the earth. Again and again and again . . .

"Chris-to-pher."

Asha-po crouched before me, his hand stilling my fist. Slowly, the tremors worked through my body until it calmed. I loosed my bloodied grip on the rock. It fell, rolling into the cold, brackish water of the marsh.

"Chris-to-pher. Earth mother not need war made on her." His face of granite cracked. Compassion replaced stone. "Earth mother sees sorrow in spirit. *I* see sorrow."

"In my very soul, Asha-po! What must I do? What *can* I do?"

He rose. "Help set traps. Coming winter bad for Sewee, bad for English, too. Earth mother punishes all so we may learn."

Asha-po was better than an almanac. A gale arrived on Christmas Day, bringing with it winds that raised heavy swells in the sea. Next came snow, riding the tail of the winds.

"Ridiculous," Father muttered. He paced the confines of our tiny hut, stranded by the weather like the rest of us. "Unheard of in these latitudes!"

Mother was more practical. "Can we not make firewood of some of that waiting lumber?"

"Before we freeze to death!" Julia wailed, shivering beneath a tent of quilts and blankets.

"There is no fireplace in the hut!" Father bellowed.

He stated the obvious. The huts had been built for temporary shelter in a tropical land. Cooking was always done outside. No one had expected true winter. I lay on my cot staring through a rack of antlers at the thatch above. "I can stand on the table and cut a hole through the thatch. Then if we move the table—"

"Where?" Father snarled.

"Outside. For the duration. If we move the table, there will be room for a fire pit—"

"Where shall we have our meals?" Mother fussed.

"On the floor, as the Sewee do." I snorted. "Not that there's much to eat."

Mother and Father both swung their heads between thatch and table, then back again, as if deliberating between civilization and barbarism.

"In heaven's name," Julia cried. "It is not that hard a decision! I'll help Christopher make the chimney hole."

◇        ◇        ◇

Asha-po was right about the deer, too. Unbeknownst to me, during my long absence our hunters—with the dangers of both the Spanish and the hostile Indians behind them—had taken to the forest and its herds with indiscriminate enthusiasm. First they had killed for meat. Next they'd killed for skins, leaving carcasses to rot in the forest. Come January, the abundance that could have fed us through the unusually harsh winter was gone. All the clam beds within miles had been raided. The lobster had migrated to deeper waters, and the constant gales kept us from fish as well as oyster beds. Flour barrels were long since empty. The emaciated livestock were slaughtered. Our small harvest of corn was fast disappearing.

The colonists of Carolina faced famine.

"What have you to say for yourself, George Culpepper?"

The colony's surveyor general stood before Father at the court which had convened within the great hall of the palisade. Most of the colonists were present, shivering beneath layers of clothing. Yes, they were angry. But it was also a rare entertainment—especially since the subject was food, currently foremost in everyone's mind. Culpepper slouched before Father's desk, his ginger hair thinner, his voice the usual whine.

"I was hungry."

"And are we not *all* hungry?" Father roared. "Is that reason enough to steal from out the very mouths of our women and children? To steal from our future?"

The weasel had been caught breaking into the barrels of spring seed. It was all that would keep us from a second year of famine. He showed no noticeable remorse.

"You have nothing more to speak in your defense?" Father prodded.

No response.

Father tugged at the wig he'd donned for the ceremonial occasion. I knew it itched. He had chosen not to shave his head as was the usual practice before wearing one. We'd all grown more comfortable with the informal styles of the colony, yet now Father contended with his wig as a symbol of England and the justice it signified.

"George Culpepper, know you the sentence for theft in England?"

"Hanging!" boomed Florence O'Sullivan with all the enthusiasm of one whose conscience was currently clear.

"Aye, hanging!" called others.

"Hang the villain!"

"No." Father leaned back in his chair. "Hanging would be too good for him." He banged his official gavel upon the desk with authority. "I sentence

George Culpepper to solitary confinement within his hut until the supply ship arrives. Let him dine until then upon water. And let him be shipped back to England in chains upon that same ship. The Lord Proprietors may deal with him."

"But my land . . ." Culpepper whimpered.

"Your rights to land in the Colony of Carolina are now and forevermore null and void." This time Father's gavel smashed the desk. "Take the prisoner away."

"Water is fine for Culpepper," Samuel Bull called out, "but 'tis hardly a punishment when the rest of us dine upon the same!"

Cries of "Aye!" filled the hall.

"What of the spring grains?" Bull pressed.

Father sighed. "If I ration out the grains, there will be no planting for the new year."

"Governor Sayle has already been lowered into the ground, and two servants buried as well. If you do not ration out the grains," Stephen Fox argued, "none of us will be alive for the spring planting."

I watched the frustration pass across Father's face. It was thinner than it had been but a month before, yet he had been eating better than most with the occasional marsh creature I'd managed to trap.

"Colonel Godfrey," he ordered at last, "after securing the prisoner, take charge of the disposition of the grain. One measure of wheat or corn for each man, woman, and child every other day—"

"Servants as well?" Godfrey inquired.

"Are they not men and women, too?" Father asked. "Must they not also eat?"

"And the demmed Westo?"

Godfrey's question stopped Father long enough for Dr. Woodward to step forward.

"If I might make a suggestion?"

Father nodded.

"Allow me to fill the sloop with as many slaves as may fit. I will attempt sailing north to Virginia. If successful, I will barter the Westo for supplies."

"Oh, aye!" the voices rose. "Well thought!"

Well thought indeed, I considered, as the doctor struck a self-congratulatory pose. Had not Woodward just completed the clearing of his own fields with his Westo? And gotten a fair start on the land of Ian Smith as well?

Father studied the crowd surrounding him for a long moment. Then he banged his gavel a final time.

"Done."

Dr. Henry Woodward, in company with Ian Smith, set sail the next morning with his cargo of slaves. The Indians were trussed and stacked like cordwood until the entire complement was packed. The sloop listed heavily in the running sea as it set out for the north. I stood watching in the cold rain, caring little for the voyage's success or failure. My sole emotion was relief.

## Nineteen

*February arrived, and along with it ice coating even* the marshes. A queer half light seemed to cause every living creature to hunker down. Their hidden lairs lay beyond my traps, beyond Asha-po's traps. The birds of the air were silenced.

The colony's hunger increased until the last well-guarded barrel of spring seeds was emptied of its final grain. Then there was nothing. In desperation, I took it upon myself to give a cookery lesson to my mother and Julia.

"Is the water boiling?" I asked, as I entered the smoky hut one foul morning.

"As fine as you please, Christopher," Julia answered.

She weakly stirred the pot over our Indian fire under our Indian chimney. It hurt me just to look at her, thin as she'd become. And there lay Mother, limp on the nearest cot, too listless to do more than give me a wan smile.

"And I added salt, too." Julia grinned. "Then I thought, what does it matter? I tossed in all the remaining herbs as well."

"A most excellent idea, little sister." I opened my pack and reached for what I had managed to forage. The point of begging from Asha-po had passed. His village was faring little better than ours. "These scraps from the tannery were not treated. They should be safe enough." I tossed in the bits of deer hide. "And—" like a magician, I pulled out my *coup*, "—one dead bird!"

"*Oooh*. Brilliant, Christopher!"

Julia lunged for the pitiful frozen pile of bones and had it cleaned in shorter order than I could have imagined. She tossed it into the pot as well. We watched the vile concoction brew until Julia painfully bent to inspect the scum frothing its edges.

"Is it done yet, Christopher?"

"It's only been a few minutes, Julia. That hide will need at least an hour."

"I'm not sure I can wait an hour, Christopher."

"You'll have to. And I will have to fetch Father, too—"

*Booooom* . . .

"What was that?" Mother propped herself up.

The thunderous sound echoed in my ears. I fear I was a little light-headed myself, else I would have considered the possibilities more rationally. It couldn't have been an alarm gun from the palisade, could it?

*Booooom!*

More thunder. Closer. Yet it was not thunder-storm season. "The Spanish?"

"*Nooo . . .*" moaned Mother.

"More Westo?" Julia squeaked.

"Heaven preserve us!" Mother prayed.

Julia stirred the mess again. "Perhaps it could be Dr. Woodward, returned from Virginia. Have you the strength to go and see, Christopher?"

"Of course." I hadn't, but I forced myself off the hard-packed sand of the floor and staggered out the door.

There was Father, running—actually *running*—through the gate of the palisade. Other colonists were showing unusual signs of life. They all seemed to be tottering toward the sea. I made my way around the hut—and there it was.

A *ship*.

A big ship, pushing through swirls of fog. I stared, then rubbed my eyes and stared some more. It was not a galleon. It was English. I watched it jockey as close to land as it possibly could. Watched anchor chains being cast into the watery depths. The fog swelled around its great bow, then cleared off once more. I squinted at the name carved and gilded upon its side: *Blessing*.

Next I fainted near dead upon the sand.

The *Blessing* brought more than our immediate salvation. Fair weather seemed to blow in upon its sails as well. Bright sun and rising temperatures graced the morrow as the colonists of Carolina—stomachs full, but still weak—spread themselves on blankets upon the sand as at an outing, watching the ship's crew unload its cargo of wonders.

We were not the only audience.

The Sewee had emerged from the forest. They gathered just clear of its edges, far less shy than at the first coming of big ships nearly a full year ago. My attention was torn between Asha-po—his lean stance as elegant as a marsh heron, his gaze as rapt—and the longboats.

First came the new colonists. They were a hundred in number, half being indentured servants. Of these servants, twenty-five arrived on their own recognizance in expectation of being hired by the original members of our settlement. Father swiftly vouched for the passage costs of three. He picked two men—one near to thirty years of age, the other closer to forty—to work on the plantation. Next he selected a young woman of perhaps eighteen or nineteen years to be Mother's promised help.

I watched my father inspect these people queued

on the shore. He did not poke or prod their muscles, as Samuel Bull did. Neither did he examine their teeth like Florence O'Sullivan. After he'd made agreements and sent them off in search of their belongings, I asked my question.

"Why did you choose those particular men, Father? Others were younger. And the woman— others had more maturity . . ."

"They had honest eyes, Christopher."

Father could hardly use the same method for selecting one of the dozen horses which next were unloaded. The longboats could not hold them, so they were lowered into the sea on hoists, then set free to thrash their way to shore. There they stamped on the sand, wet and frenzied, till they could be caught and subdued. Father chose a mare that looked strong, yet spirited. After attaching a lead to her head collar, he handed the rope to me. "You had best accustom yourself to the creature, Christopher, as she will be in your charge."

"Me?"

I had no time to say my thanks for this unexpected boon before the creature tossed her great neck, nearly tearing the lead from my grasp—and my shoulders from their sockets. I hung on in terror. Yes, I'd seen horses daily on the streets of London, but our family had never kept them, and my education had never extended to the care and feeding and *gen-*

176

*tling* of such beasts. The mare arched her entire body of a sudden, front legs kicking at the air, her very skin quivering. She let out a long whinny of fright worse than mine as I jerked back from her sharp hooves, from the near ton of power descending with them.

"Here, now."

A deep voice and strong hands brought my delivery. The rope slipped from my grip into the stranger's.

"Here, now, Mistress Folly."

I spun. The words were not for me, but for the horse, and they came from the younger of the two men Father had just hired. In but a moment, his soft croons had calmed the brute. He stood comfortably next to it, stroking the chestnut neck.

"Thank you." My breath returned. The beat of my heart slowed. "I'm Christopher, Christopher West, and I fear I know little of horses—"

"It can be taught. I cared for this beauty aboard ship."

He smiled, and I liked the look of his face. It was broad and honest, as Father had said.

"I be Ethan Browe, Master Christopher. At your service."

I smiled back. "Only for the next five years."

"Aye. Much knowledge can be gained in five years."

I nodded agreement. Think what I had learned in only one. Ethan Browe walked Folly away, taking some of my burdens with him. The fields waiting on the bluff above the Ashley River suddenly seemed almost hospitable to me.

By sunset it became obvious why the Sewee still waited so patiently. I went to my father.

"Sir—"

He straightened from the barrels and cases of goods yet to be transported to the safety of the palisade. "What is it, Christopher?"

I gestured toward the mass of Indians. With the falling shadows they were blending back into the forest again. "They wait for their warrior gifts."

"From the Westo War?"

"Of course, from the Westo War! They have been more than patient, Father. And they are hungry, too."

A harried look strayed across his face. "It will be some days before we can sort out our new supply of tools and trade goods—"

"I believe their patience has its limits, Father."

"Enough! Convey my respects to their chief and medicine man. Beg their continued patience. And—" he stooped to separate several barrels from the lot before him, "—sweeten the request with this gift. Ship biscuit and bully beef. It should fill their stomachs as well as it has ours."

I set off for Asha-po, praying that the Sewee's present of biscuit be not filled with weevils, that their barrel of bully beef be not gifted with maggots.

*Twenty*

*There were not enough tools to pay our debt of* honor to the Sewee. Naturally, I was chosen as the bearer of ill tidings. I found Asha-po where I had expected to, under our old, lone palm. Also as expected, he was deep in contemplation of the anchored ship. I offered my sorry tale, then—

"Please try to understand, Asha-po. Please try to make Sipio and Kenato understand." I bowed my head, knowing as Shakespeare had that "the first bringer of unwelcome news hath but a losing office."

Asha-po tore his attention from the sea to give me a sphinxlike look. "Explain so *I* may understand."

I ran my hand through my hair, its length now caught in a tail by a strip of rawhide. Where to begin? At the beginning. "When the last big ships sailed away from here to England—"

"The *Caroline*. The *Port Royal*," he recited.

"Yes. Those ships carried with them messages from my father. Messages that ordered more supplies. But . . ." I hesitated, " . . . these messages sailed *before* our war with the Spanish, *before* our war with the Westo. The Sewee gifts were not ordered then."

Asha-po considered. "Big ships not see fighting over Great Water."

So far, so good. I proceeded. "As you already know, it takes many moons, many months for big ships to cross the Great Water to England. Meanwhile, in England, the English people worry for us living here. They worry that maybe the food is not enough—"

"Maybe harvest is bad," Asha-po offered.

"Yes, as it happened. So our English friends sent the *new* big ship, the *Blessing*, before the *Caroline* and the *Port Royal* finished their voyages back across the ocean."

"New big ship not see fighting, either."

"No. The ocean is very large." I caught my friend's eyes. "Asha-po. My father sends new messages with the *Blessing*. The ship will set sail again soon. These new messages tell the king himself of the great courage of the Sewee. They tell of the aid your people have given to us. They order the gifts that have been promised."

"No tools come with the *Blessing*? No knives?"

Here was the hardest part. "Well, yes. But only some. Only enough for the new English."

"*More* English." Asha-po spat.

"Please. They might resemble us, but perhaps they will do better." I reached behind for the sack I'd brought to our meeting. Out of it I pulled a hoe and a knife. "These I found for your family." I studied the objects. These I'd *stolen* from the palisade store. I offered them.

Asha-po shoved them back.

"Why?"

"My father use steel knife, Sewee men say, 'Where is *my* steel knife?' My mother use iron hoe, Sewee women say, 'Where is *my* iron hoe?'"

"Of course." How foolish of me. I bundled up the spurned gifts. Even the Sewee knew jealousy. Even the Sewee could covet. Were they not human, too? I grabbed the sack and turned to leave our old meeting place. Asha-po stopped me.

"Chris-to-pher. The *Blessing* sails four . . . five . . . maybe *six* moons till it finds England." He held up the fingers, then counted them a second time. "It sails four . . . five . . . maybe *six* moons before it comes again. Planting time passes. Time of heat passes. Harvest passes. Cold comes again."

"Yes." I shrugged helplessly. "It could be a full year."

"A new year Sewee plant with sticks. A new year

Sewee chip stone for knife, chip stone for hatchet not so sharp as English."

I sighed.

"Sewee grow old," Asha-po continued. "*I* grow old. Take wife. Watch wife poke ground with stick. Make son. Watch son hunt with stone. Maybe English king never send Sewee gifts. Maybe English ship never comes."

"Asha-po, I swear before God—"

He held up his hand to halt my oath. "English god not sun father, not earth mother. How English god know Sewee needs?" He broke away from the sea and strode back into the forest.

Very shortly thereafter the Sewee began building canoes. *Huge* canoes. I wanted to ask Asha-po *why*, but pride held me back. Had he not scorned my offerings? Had he not broken our friendship by stubbornly refusing to give any weight to the problems of the English? Instead I spied on the work from within the denseness of the forest, like a Westo scout on an intelligence-gathering mission. Yet very soon I myself was too busy to either spy or wonder.

Bolstered by the new colonists—and especially by the new servants—the little English village by the sea was rapidly dispersing inland to take possession of the lands it claimed by authority of King Charles II and his Lord Proprietors. The *Blessing* hauled anchor and set sail on its return voyage, heavy with its cargo of timber for English shipbuilders and hides to be crafted into English breeches. With the help of myself and of our horse, Ethan Browe and James Long—Father's older servant of choice—cleared a trail to the West plantation. Upon its completion, Mother and Julia in company with Milly Harris, our new maidservant, joined Father and me. The West family took up residence in its manor house at last.

Having regained her strength, and having accepted the inevitable, Mother set about becoming the mistress of the manor.

"Joseph," she proclaimed at the very first formal meal in our new dining room. "Joseph. I cannot live with these rough-boarded walls."

Father extricated his attention from his tankard of ale—another boon of the *Blessing* which had raised his spirits considerably—to study the walls. "The joints are set very tightly, my dear. Not a bad piece of carpentry, all things considered."

"But our house in London had *plaster* on its walls."

"And where am I to get *plaster*, pray tell?"

I watched the look passing between my parents. It was a familiar one, shortly to be followed by a lessening in good humor on both their parts. I raised my knife for attention.

"You know that mound of shells near the river?"

Father sniffed. "Years of garbage from your Indians."

I ignored the jibe. "Ethan Browe says it can easily be burned into lime. Lime is what is used for plaster and whitewash, is it not?"

"Christopher!" Mother smiled on me with even greater favor than usual. "After the inner walls be plastered, we could whitewash the outside as well—"

"Then it really would look like a great manor house!" Julia beamed.

"Save your enthusiasm, ladies. Both of you." Father offered *his* favor to the waiting ale. We all waited for him to brush his lips with his napkin. "With the planting hardly begun, there is little time for cosmetics."

"But," I pointed out, "Ethan Browe says that lime would also be useful to spread on our fields, since they could use all the enrichment we can give them. And he knows the building of limekilns—"

"Ethan Browe, Ethan Browe," Father muttered. He notched up his voice. "It's all I ever hear. Can the man do no wrong?"

Milly—plump and cheerful as ever—entered at this juncture with a laden tray. "Ethan Browe?" her color rose. "The very salt of the earth. A man who can be relied upon. Would you be wanting your pudding now?"

Ethan Browe and I built the limekiln. In truth, Ethan did most of the work with the strength and patience of a blacksmith, while I learned. Mother got her plaster and whitewash. After the success of these improvements, she began making lists for critical items to be ordered by next ship: china, fine furniture, a harpsichord. Her plastered rooms would be filled with the luxuries of London. Father was wise enough not to question the cost of these luxuries. The next ship would be a long time coming. It was enough that Mother was content with her dreams.

Julia spent most of her days helping Milly. It did not appear to be a sacrifice. As I passed the kitchen I often heard them singing rounds of "Summer Is Icumin In," or "Now Robin Lend to Me Thy Bow." Other times I heard a steady stream of gossip and laughter. Some of the gossip my sister chose to share with me as I delivered firewood or a pail of water.

"Milly took passage of a broken heart, Christopher. She was left standing at the very altar! So sad, so romantic . . ." A deep sigh.

I would leave my sister to her sighs till the next encounter.

"We suspect James Long of some dark deed, secretive as he is, but we must ponder its nature. Theft?" She shook her head before I could protest. "He appears not the least dishonest. Maybe something political. He *is* dour enough to have been a Roundhead. . . ."

James Long a follower of Oliver Cromwell?

Responsible for the beheading of Charles I? Perhaps. I would trot back to the fields to mull over the thought, and returning, find my sister's tongue still wagging like an old crone.

"As for Ethan Browe—"

"Enough!" I'd not have my new hero slandered.

"Christopher!" Julia's chatter stopped cold. "You sound just like Father!"

I grinned and took my leave. I would meet my sister again soon enough. She spent all of her free time with our mare, Folly, and was included in the grooming and riding lessons Ethan also dispensed.

Secretive he might be, but the dark and wiry James Long was also useful. I allowed him his silences, particularly as his competence increasingly seemed to lie in farming. I had carefully explained to him the significance of corn, and he had just as carefully listened. By late April most of our fields had been plowed with Folly's help, and half of them sown with corn that had belatedly arrived from Virginia with Dr. Henry Woodward and the sloop. Our family's share bore far more promise for me than the lost labor of the Westo who had paid so dearly for it. By May, Long was experimenting on the remainder of the fields with samples that had come with the *Blessing*: indigo and sugar cane and cotton by way of Barbados.

"What, no wheat?" I asked him one day.

"Wheat in Carolina be folly and waste. The soil will not countenance it."

They were the longest two sentences I'd had from the man. They were also the most telling. I gave over all future crop decisions to him with confidence and a lighter heart.

Thus matters stood as spring seemingly flew into the summer of 1671, into the summer of our second year in Carolina. Tentatively we made new decisions based upon the errors of the past. More than tentatively the wilderness was being tamed. Early one mid-June morning I stood back and surveyed the West fields. The corn was rising so fast its arms already passed the stumps of ravaged trees, nearly hiding them. The arms of the corn. There was something about that image . . .

> *Corn will rise up standing;*
> *to all directions*
> *Will it stretch its arms,*
> *That Sewee may always live.*

Kenato's blessing song returned. It returned with such intensity that I staggered.

*Asha-po.*

The plantation's work had filled my every waking moment for months. It was only during the long darkness of the night that I allowed myself to think of my old friend. My first friend in this new land. Wrapped in the loneliness of that same darkness, I prayed for his return with greater intensity than ever I had for my brother Jonathan's fellowship.

*Asha-po.*

The need to see my friend overcame me with a suddenness beyond understanding. Sewee pride had turned Asha-po against me. I had been prideful, too. It was English pride that had sustained me after he'd walked away that last time. English pride had kept me hidden within the forest as he redirected his energies to the building of his great canoe. *Pride.* I suddenly understood the deadliest of the Seven Deadly Sins as no catechism could ever teach me.

I raced to where Folly was grazing. Saddled the mare with urgency. Set myself astride.

"Christopher!" Julia skipped out of the kitchen house. "I was just about to bring in breakfast—"

"I can't wait. I have an errand in the village."

"But no one is there!"

I stared down her protest.

"You will be back this evening, Christopher? It's Midsummer Night! Milly and I have planned a celebration. Christopher, you *know* the Bulls are coming for their first visit, and that new Mathews family—"

I kicked Folly. Little suspecting the kick was

coming, she bolted. We galloped across the edge of
the fields and onto the narrow trail to the sea.

Folly was in a lather when I pulled back the reins at
the end of the trail, by the edge of the forest. I drew
an arm across my face, wiping away my own sweat.
My eyes cleared. But maybe they hadn't. I swiped at
them again. The vision before me was too unbeliev-
able.

Spread out across the sea were Sewee canoes.
*Huge* Sewee canoes. They were laden with Indians
and their belongings. Laden with the *entire tribe.* I
watched the gargantuan canoes jockey for position
until every prow faced east, as if for a grand regatta.
East toward the still-ascending sun. East toward the
vast Atlantic. My breath caught within me, and for a
moment I could only stare at the boats, the calm sea,
the brilliance of the sky above all.

*Zoons.*

It couldn't be. It was not possible. The auda-
ciousness of the undertaking hit like a hammer
blow. I dug my boots into poor Folly's flanks yet
again, and she careened down to the sea. I drove
her past deserted huts, across hard sand, and
straight into the waves. As if knowing, the creature
led me past several idling boats, then stopped when
the water reached her withers. Stopped next to
Asha-po's canoe.

His paddle was raised in his hand, his attention focused on the leading canoe. Kenato was loftily balanced within it, communing with the sun.

"Asha-po—"

He turned and lowered the paddle. "Chris-to-pher."

"Asha-po. You would leave without telling me? Without my knowing?"

He touched his heart. "I send message with earth mother. I feel your knowing."

It was so. The corn had spoken to me. What, then, was left?

"Asha-po. Will you forgive me?"

A smile touched his lips. "What to forgive, Chris-to-pher? You try to be Sewee. Not work. I think hard, think what *will* work. Think maybe Sewee try to be English. Try to be *best* part of English."

He gestured at the flotilla.

"We build big ships. We journey across Great Water. We find English king. Show courage of Sewee." He stopped. His face hardened into its granite look.

"We carry back tools. We carry back horses. We carry back *guns*. With these . . . maybe we bring back deer, bring back trees, bring back old Sewee land."

"Asha-po," I begged. "The voyage is too long. You have no sails—" I stopped before speaking the most obvious truth. *You cannot carry back the past.*

Ahead of us, Kenato ended his prayer to the sun father. He settled within his canoe and readied his paddle. Then he sang out a chant.

"*Yai, ne, noo, way. E, noo, way **hah**!*"

The warriors picked up the chant in rhythm. Asha-po's voice joined them. Strong. Resolute.

"*Yai, ne, noo, way. E, noo, way **hah**!*"

"Asha-po!" I cried.

He turned a last time. "A *friend* you seem to be."

I wiped sea spray from my face. Perhaps it was not sea spray.

"*Brothers* I think we are, despite all," I said.

Asha-po nodded a final nod of acceptance and plowed the blade of his paddle into the sea.

I sat astride Folly, letting the water wash over us both till the great canoes of the Sewee disappeared over the horizon on their impossible voyage. Only then did I nudge Folly ashore to the Eden the Sewee had abandoned. The empty forest waited in silence before me.

# 21
## Twenty-one

*Midsummer Night is the longest day of the year.*
After the sun father blazed out in glory, a monstrous
hurricane swept into Carolina from the sea. The
manor house stood firm. The Sewee never returned.

# AUTHOR'S NOTE

The Sewee are one of the lost tribes of the Carolinas. Their extinction did not come as a result of the usual ravages of European disease or conflict. The Sewee disappeared as described in this novel. It is a curious tale which left me feeling wrenched the moment I unearthed it. Making the discovery wasn't easy, for the primary reference to these people in colonial literature consists of several scant paragraphs in John Lawson's 1709 *A New Voyage to Carolina*. Today the sole archeological remains of the Sewee include a stone ring, which points out their distinctive form of sun worship, and the shell middens they left behind.

To tell the Sewee's story, I felt it was necessary to tell the story of the first English who arrived in Carolina in 1670. They paid the small fortune of five pounds each to be cast off on a voyage as treacherous as any contemporary one to the moon. They came because they succumbed to the period's get-rich-quick promotional land pamphlets which described Carolina as:

> the most amiable Country of the Universe . . . Nature has not bless'd the World with any Tract, which can be preferable to it, that *Paradise*, with all her Virgin Beauties, may be modestly suppos'd at most but equal to its Native Excellencies.

The pamphleteers had never made the voyage, had never seen the land.

With a grasp of the English emigrants' mind-set, I then worked from period descriptions and lists of passengers of the original ships. Although fictionalized by necessity, the English who took part in this adventure were *real*. Children accompanying their parents were rarely named, so Christopher West may or may not have actually existed. His father did. Joseph West was the moving force behind the struggling settlement and was named temporary governor several times in the early years of Carolina. Among the other authentic characters, Dr. Henry Woodward alternately traded with and enslaved the Indians. Florence O'Sullivan deserted the post on his island namesake. And Mr. Culpepper was, indeed, later returned to England to be tried for treasonable conspiracies against the colony.